FIRE, BU

Chris Crowcroft

St Lawrence's, Ludlow

FIRE, BURN!

Chris Crowcroft

A Second Case for Richard Palmer, Investigator

AESOP Modern
Oxford

AESOP Modern
An imprint of AESOP Publications
Martin Noble Editorial / AESOP
28 Abberbury Road, Oxford OX4 4ES, UK
www.aesopbooks.com

First edition published by AESOP Publications
Copyright (c) 2016 Chris Crowcroft

A catalogue record of this book is
available from the British Library.

First edition 2016

ISBN: 978-1-910301-34-0

Printed and bound in Great Britain by
Lightning Source UK Ltd,
Chapter House, Pitfield, Kiln Farm,
Milton Keynes MK11 3LW

Reviews of Palmer's first case: Shakespeare in Trouble

'A stunning debut'   *John McLaren*

'A must-read'   *Peter Bassano*

'An intriguing twist on the Shakespeare tale'
      Simon Tait, ai magazine

'May we see Palmer on another case? I hope so'
      Andy Sawyer, Foundation

For those who wanted to see Richard Palmer
on the case again

Note: dates used obey the modern calendar not the old, when the year changed after March 25th.

Chris Crowcroft
chris@crowcroft.co.uk

COULD THE END justify the means?

The words of a warm June evening in the house by the river forced their way back into the mind of the mild Jesuit priest. He saw the questioner in his mind's eye, tall, forceful to the point of fanatical in the faith, a leader of men where he, the priest, was not.

'If it were for the good of our faith, Father, would it be right that innocent people might die ... in destroying the guilty?'

He should have realised that the words were chosen too carefully to be of the moment, that they must have been rehearsed. What had he answered? He couldn't pretend to forget, despite the glass of wine too many at the time. He wished he hadn't said what he did, about 'those caught in the middle having to accept the fortunes of war'. Whatever had he been thinking?

He felt again that awful sense of foreboding which had crept over him when the man had left, abruptly, as if he had been given the key to something important.

Robin Catesby...

... the most dangerous type of believer, Father Henry Garnet admitted to himself, sincere to the point of rashness. The loss of a young wife hadn't helped, the priest reflected as he toyed with his rosary; it had only inflamed Catesby's readiness to act regardless of the consequences.

He sighed – he should have known better, better than to be carried away by this warrior for the faith. Catesby was doubly dangerous, and why? Because he had the charisma to draw the naive into his enthusiasm. Enthusiasm for what? For crusade, there was no other word for it. Catesby was a zealot, a man for action *now,* for instant revolution. Gradualism and the patience of politics, which was the priest's way, held no appeal for such as Catesby.

'I'm done with waiting.' That was what Catesby had said.

Garnet tried to draw comfort from his attempt to confront the man in the days after this unfortunate encounter. Had it had any effect? He remembered now what Catesby had said then in an attempt to deflect him.

'I have so much to tell you about the great work we have in hand.'

Great work? What was it Catesby was trying to do?

To convert him to violence? And he a priest! He shook his head at the memory – he had refused to be told, he didn't want to know, he begged for caution. He thought he had succeeded.

Today that fear was completing its terrible circle back to him.

'Be clear, what is it you want from me?'

The bark in his question was uncharacteristic. Father Oswald Tesimond, the man to whom it was addressed, was momentarily surprised by it. Were long years of mission to the apostate English at last proving too much for his superior? Was he hoping for a return to the quieter life of prayer in Rome? How would he stand up to interrogation if the English Government ever caught him?

Tesimond got straight to the point.

'What I have to say concerns something Catesby told me in confession.'

'Then it is sealed by the privacy of the confessional'.

'No!'

'No?'

Garnet was reproachful. He knew that the younger priest sympathised with the men of action, the firebrands like Robin

Catesby from Stratford. If Tesimond was disturbed, then matters were very serious indeed.

Tesimond adjusted his manner, lowering his voice to a more respectful tone.

'I have come to confess and to seek advice,' he said. 'In confessing to me, Catesby has agreed that I can share his confession with you.'

Garnet's relief grew. Confession bound him to justifiable silence afterwards, or so he believed. He watched Tesimond begin to kneel before him.

'Not here,' he urged him, as if the walls of the room might have ears. 'Let's walk outside.'

The garden was placid, airless, suffocated by the heat of summer. The only noise was a buzzing of insects. It was a little Eden, one about to be shattered by what Tesimond had to say. Garnet's reaction was incredulous.

'Blow the King up when he opens Parliament! Has Catesby lost his mind?'

The flames of hellfire roared in his ears and burned his scorching cheeks. It was beyond his wildest fears. Yes, Catesby was planning something, that much he knew, but this, to assassinate the King and all his Government!

The revelation robbed Garnet of what little breath the stifling heat allowed. The sweat which began to soak the chemise of the older man had nothing to do with the temperature of the day. He repeated in disbelief what Tesimond had told him as if it were a horrible fantasy.

'Blow the King up?'

His mind raced over all that would be put at risk by such lunacy – his years of underground ministry which had comforted the faithful and brought back thousands to the Catholic flock; the possibility for a new tolerance of the faith by the State under a new monarch....

'Words, just words,' was what Catesby reckoned about King James's hazy promises to English Catholics. Catesby wanted more, much more. A collision was on course if both sides weren't careful, in Garnet's fearful opinion. It was everything the priest had worked to avoid.

'What can we do?' he heard himself say to Tesimond. He was past knowing. This huge leap, from disobedience to terror, defeated his skill to respond to it.

Men had been recruited, work was underway?

Did he hear right what Tesimond was telling him, that they were hoping to wipe out the entire Government and all its supporters in the blast? And that others might die too, moderates, good Catholics some of them, simply for being in the wrong place at the wrong time? *That*, Garnet now realised, that had been the point of Catesby's riverside question. He thrust the palm of his hand angrily against his forehead.

'It's no more than Papal policy,' Tesimond said, careful to report it as Catesby's claim, 'the policy which brought us Jesuit fathers back into England in the first place, to bring England back to the true faith. Elizabeth was no legitimate ruler, nor is her Protestant successor James...'

... for all that the King's martyred mother Mary had been a devout Catholic.

Garnet sighed. The policy was old, there was a new Holy Father. Who knew what he thought? His body and mind ached for retirement. Shocks such as this affected him physically these days – the sweating and the queasiness, the inability to think clearly. He was getting too old for it. Past fears, of capture, trial and horrible execution began to resurface in his mind along with the old question – would he have the courage to endure them? And what did Tesimond expect from him? Was he on the side of the angry young men too?

He was suddenly aware of the heat in the garden. He wanted the cool, he wanted sanctuary.

'We should contact Rome,' Tesimond said.

'Yes,' Garnet agreed, clutching at straws. 'I really believe we must.'

Slumped in the back room of the Bell Inn hard by St Paul's Cathedral in the City of London, Richard Palmer was not a happy man.

'Last one, no more money,' he grumbled to himself, swishing an inch of liquor around in the pot in front of him.

Times were thin for the investigator. His slate in the tavern was beyond his pocket to settle. His last job was in limbo after yet another outbreak of the plague in the capital.

There was only one consolation.

'At least I'm spared the plays on Bankside,' he muttered.

The Alderman's young wife he'd been trailing, she couldn't get enough of these plays but now the theatres were closed because of the contagion. The Alderman and his wife had decamped from the capital. As it was, he'd already been forced to sit through the roarings of a blacked-up stage general jealous to the point of madness over a pale young wife. His only consolation was the name of his old flame, Emilia, given to a waiting woman onstage. It would not have pleased her! The modern drama got no better for him by repetition, exactly the opposite.

He saw the landlord approach. He was running out of excuses over the money he owed him. He was feeling rough enough as it was and talking to himself, never a good sign.

The landlord took a stool and pulled it up close. Palmer waited for the inevitable word about his slate. What he heard instead surprised him.

'Been someone here, askin' after you. Looked official, smelled o' Whitehall to me,' the landlord said, referring to the sprawling seat of Government less than a mile to the west. 'Said you should report in, Government business, you'd know where to go.'

It could only mean Lord Salisbury, Robert Cecil as was, Palmer felt sure. He'd once taken an assignment from the Chief Minister in the time of the old Queen, Elizabeth, following a writer and a trail of sonnets. William Shakespeare had wriggled free.

Palmer wasn't feeling well and the memory made him no better.

The landlord saw it too.

'Best get yourself off 'ome, Dick,' he said, pulling his stool away.

Palmer barely made it back to his chamber in the Clerkenwell tenement. The final stairs almost finished him. An appalling intimation throbbed in his sickening brain. There was no-one he could call, he was on his own.

He collapsed, half conscious, into the bed.

He had no energy to pull his clothes off. He did not want to see what his nakedness would reveal. His head was on fire, he was burning up, it was difficult to breathe or to control the trembling which was spreading throughout his body. He could feel angry swellings under his arms and in his groin. He dimly understood what was to follow, he'd seen it before – the scorching fever and the racking pain and the vomiting and the bursting of the boils already throbbing to the point where they would explode and ooze the terrible, stinking slime of black death.

He needed water, buckets of it. There was a pitcher on a sideboard. He knew he had as much chance of reaching it as flying to the moon.

He faded into a merciful unconsciousness...

It was in the othertime, in the depths of the night when Palmer came round.

He was not sure whether he was dead or alive. As his eyes adjusted to the dark, he recognised where he was. He could barely move from weakness. He smelled the pungent odour of the sweat of sickness and other bodily evacuations permeating his clothes. When he tried to move, they stuck clammily to him.

With a massive effort he turned from his front onto his side. He was alive! He tried to take off his clothes. It was more than he could manage. He rested. How long had he been like this? Hours? Days? He felt the tender parts of his body. The swelling was less.

Feebly his fingers began to function so that he could loosen his clothes. Was this the lull before the fatal quietus of the disease? His breathing came more easily. He began to guess that he was going to live after all.

He desperately needed water. He thought about crying out, or croaking. He stopped himself – if anyone came they would see how he was and avoid him, yes, well, like the plague. Intrusion only meant danger, at best incarceration with the damning circle painted up on his door. He made himself wait, and sleep a little more.

Bright light greeted his second return to consciousness, followed by noise from the street outside and the dinning of rival church bells. He counted seven clanging chimes from the church nearby. He rolled off the bed and crawled towards the sideboard, levering himself up towards the pitcher of water. With one hand he made it topple towards him, splashing his face. He hauled the pitcher down, consuming the musty contents in one long gulp.

~ 2 ~

THREE DAYS passed before Palmer was fit enough to follow up the message left for him to report to Whitehall.

He went there by boat along the Thames, the main thoroughfare in the capital where the streets were slow, dirty and downright dangerous. The water took the edge off the ferocious summer heat while the journey rested his weakened body. To prevent conversation he turned his back on his waterman. He was dressed in his better suit, the only suit now that he had burned the sickness-stained working clothes. It hung off him.

Arriving on the north bank at Whitehall stairs in the heart of Government, he found his way to the outer chamber of the great man he was looking for.

An official answered testily when Palmer asked him if the Chief Minister was still in town, waving at the busy room around them. Parliament was still sitting, even if the present monarch was starting to show signs of disrespect for it. The Stuart style, men said, was a direct line to God for authority and to Parliament for cash.

With permission he passed on into a smaller chamber controlled by the veteran official who knew him and knew his business.

'Where have you been? The Chief Minister has been asking for you for days.'

Palmer was told to wait, for some hours if necessary.

He sat down and began to doze while appearing to be awake, an old trick.

'Richard Palmer!'

At last! He pulled himself together at the sound of the summons, took a deep breath and stifled the husky reaction in his lungs. The Chief Minister was the sharpest knife in the box – he had to be, after a decade in power under Elizabeth and now James. Palmer was on his mettle to perform well. Well was not how he felt.

He got up and followed the official to his appointment.

The room where Salisbury sat, head bent over piles of papers was familiar to Palmer. So was its occupant, yet changed too.

What surprised Palmer were the depth of the lines on the politician's face and the grey hair infiltrating his hair and beard. Power aged some men as much as poverty did others, he reminded himself.

'Good to see you,' the Chief Minister said. 'Are you well?'

Palmer's old, new suit felt uncomfortably loose after his recent experiment with death. Did it made him look lean and determined? He restricted himself to a smile of acknowledgement. He had visions of a jingling bag of silver coming, of the good times returning.

The question Salisbury put to him almost threw him off guard.

'You come from a Catholic family, I believe, and a recusant one too?'

Palmer's brain screamed caution.

'Catholic ... recusant,' these were dangerous labels to admit to.

'My father....' Palmer began by way of excuse.

His father had been the recusant, not him, refusing to change his religion with the fashion of the times; worse, refusing to attend the new rite at all. It had cost the family everything when the fines for recusancy were increased a hundredfold. Why couldn't the old man have followed his faith in private and shut his mouth in public? It was the way of plenty of others.

Salisbury forestalled him.

'It could prove very useful ... in the coming times'.

'Are difficulties expected?' Palmer asked.

Salisbury gave him a look of faint amusement.

'There are always difficulties.'

Palmer waited patiently. Salisbury spoke.

'A minority of Catholics has never accepted our secession from Rome. Most of these accept the disadvantages which follow. Those disadvantages have gone up or down according to the political climate, would you not say?'

Palmer shrugged. In the case of the Palmer family, 'disadvantage' had meant total expropriation. Monthly fines were more than the average man earned in years.

'His Majesty at first intended a more relaxed approach to Catholic concerns,' Salisbury went on. 'Perhaps this gave them too much hope.'

What the King offered was words, not change, both men knew. Disappointment was inevitable. It would have been better not to give hope in the first place, to let it be *understood*. Tolerance, of which the King spoke, was not the same as toleration, a legal act.

'Difficulties are always with us,' Salisbury said. 'Government is being forced to ply a hazardous course, between two militant and opposing tendencies, those of the old faith who want to return to the past, and those of the new, who want religious practice in its most radical form.'

Calvin, Knox, no bishops, no intervening priest, Palmer understood at once who, like the majority, couldn't care less and who, like the majority was ignored by the extremists at both ends driven on by the faith burning in their hearts. It was another reason why he spent his Sundays avoiding the church service which the Law demanded.

'We are hearing worrying reports from our people on the continent, from Brussels in particular. We are not sure what is going on – we are of course at peace with Spain, and in the Low Countries. Our fear is conspiracy.'

'*Catholic* conspiracy ?' Palmer cut in.

Salisbury gave him a long, hard look.

'Of course,' he said at last.

'How can I ... help?'

Palmer was beginning to feel light-headed, as if his mind was leaving his body. He wasn't well. He hoped Salisbury did not notice.

'I have nothing specific in mind. My fear is another attempt against the King, altogether more serious than the last ones – the intelligence we are getting is unclear. Of course, all our regular informers are working hard on it. Even so, I think it would be wise to apply extra, independent effort, reporting directly to me – you did a good job for me once before.'

Four years ago, that trail of sonnets between a fashionable playwright and his treasonous patron, since when not a word, not a crumb. Palmer maintained his look of careful attention.

'I may need you – not just yet, I will decide when – to penetrate the Jesuit underground.'

Salisbury looked keenly over at Palmer. Palmer gave a nod of acceptance.

'For the time being, act on your own initiative, run your eye over the usual suspects, sniff around, take the temperature of what is or isn't going on. There is a writer we are not sure about,' Salisbury said as if it was a last, less important thought, 'a Catholic convert and a recusant, a convicted killer....'

Palmer raised an eyebrow.

'... Ben Jonson – do you know him? No? He writes for The King's Men – you would have known them as the Lord Chamberlain's Men under our late Queen.'

Palmer had, and their leading man William Shakespeare. Shakespeare was lucky that his head was still joined to his shoulders, in Palmer's opinion. It was just like the man to come up smelling of rosewater. He heard Salisbury out.

'Ben Jonson has form, he spent time in prison over one of his plays – "conspiracy against the Emperor" type of plot, so easy to send the wrong message if you are not careful ... and care is not Jonson's style. He has switched to these new entertainments Queen Anne is so fond of, the masques in which she dances. They give him worrying *access* to Their Majesties in person.'

'Is he a serious suspect?'

'I do hope not – he has been trying to secure my patronage; I would be embarrassed if he was planning regicide.'

Palmer made to leave. Salisbury detained him with one more thought.

'Keep the best-known Catholic peers in mind. Something tells me that the key to what is going on lies in that old circle of mischief. It is the larger animals, not the smaller we should fear.'

Clutching a well-filled purse, Palmer was being led out by the old official when a face in the crowd outside stopped him in his tracks.

'Isn't that Lanier?' he asked.

The official nodded his head.

'Well, well,' Palmer said, 'a change in the weather makes friends of us all.'

Alphonse Lanier had been mixed up in riot and revolution in the last years of the old Queen. He was another one Palmer reckoned was lucky to have survived.

'Captain Lanier is in receipt of a government perquisite,' the old official told him.

Something to do with a sixpenny surcharge for the weighing of hay.

'... although he has yet to get the money. Grant and receipt are quite different things to our Scottish colleagues,' the old public servant said with a cynical smile.

It was yet another example of gravy for the undeserving, to Palmer's mind, and the need to lodge your tongue deep up the crevice of the powers-that-be. He looked Lanier over once more. The man's bent nose gave him satisfaction – his last encounter with the man had left an enduring mark. But what about his wife? What about Emilia?

'Wasn't Mrs Lanier the mistress of the Lord Chamberlain, the old one?' he asked, perfectly aware that she was and searching for news.

The official was forthcoming.

'She lives away from her husband, in the country with Lady Cumberland and her daughter. It is an especially *devout* household.'

Emilia turning to religion? Palmer smiled at the thought.

The passage by boat down the Thames put Palmer into a rare good mood. He tolerated conversation from his waterman, keen to tell him that the places of public entertainment on the other side of the river had been closed on account of plague. Palmer shivered at his own brush with the infection.

'You're an educated man, sir', the waterman said, 'what d'you think causes it?'

'I have no idea,' Palmer said.

'Me neither,' the waterman admitted. 'I think the better air out 'ere on the water 'elps, leastwise till it gets up to the reg'lar midsummer stink. Me? I carries me old lucky charm.'

Palmer smiled at such superstition, which no amount of religion would replace. And who was to say, if it made the waterman think he was protected, that he wasn't? It made as much sense to Palmer as medical rigmaroles which only doctors understood, or their foul compounds.

'You goin' to Bankside for the playhouses?' the waterman asked.

Palmer confirmed it. He was thinking of starting with the playwriter Jonson.

'You won't find nobody there. Closed as I said, on account o' the plague. You lookin' for someone in partic'lar?' The waterman knew where he had picked his fare up from, Whitehall, the kennel of Government and its hounds. This man looked just like one, of the mongrel variety.

Palmer threw out the name of Ben Jonson.

The waterman beamed.

'Funny you should mention 'im. Can't say as I knows 'im, but I knows where 'e drinks, cos it's where I do – the Mermaid in....'

'Bread Street?' Palmer knew his London drinking holes.

'That's right, off Thames Street. 'Course I can't say as 'e'll be there, but it might be worth checkin' out. You wanna go there now? Right-o ... .means pullin' back to the north bank again.'

Palmer grimaced at the hint. He offered the waterman a few coppers more, the ones which had been his last few until Salisbury put him back into harness.

~ 3 ~

ADOZEN MILES north, out in open country on the Barnet road, a single rider was pushing his horse into a brisk trot.

Robin Catesby was making for Father Garnet's safehouse in Enfield. He had a great deal on his mind. By now Garnet would know his intention from Tesimond. There would be pressure from the Jesuit, pressure on him to give up his plan.

'For this I was made,' Catesby repeated to himself.

The words, spoken like a catechism, brought on a deep calm which was, to him, a sure sign of his direction and purpose. They could only be ordained by God.

It didn't last. His very human anger intervened.

Cut off the head of the monster James! Cut it off even if the slayer died in the process – life on earth was vanity – only, do it in such a way that it would be seen to be worth dying for. Hurl the flames of hell at the infidel usurper like an avenging deity! He had no fear of death. Beyond this life Kate was waiting for him, his wife in heaven....

The shrill chirruping of a flock birds overhead brought him back down to earth. Garnet would have to be put off, he decided. If only the Jesuit superior had the guts of priests like Tesimond. Tesimond had spirit, Tesimond was a fighter. Garnet? He was a conciliator with Caesar not a warrior for Christ. The time for compromise was over, or for believing in the lies of politicians.

And how well the plan was developing! Finding a vault for hire right under the Parliament chamber, surely it was a sign? The gunpowder, thirty odd barrels of it – enough to blow Parliament up several times over according to his man Fawkes

– was already safe inside, stored, ready, waiting. They would blow to hell King, Government and all the leaders of the Protestant heresy so providentially assembled in one place!

Excitement at the image transmitted to his limbs which spurred his horse into a canter.

His only real worry was money. His horse slowed.

Money!

God's work needed money. There was the house near Parliament to pay for, for longer than they had thought, and the explosives which Fawkes insisted they must continue to check were fit for purpose; it would cost if they had to replace them. And the men involved cost money too.

Well, he would sell his home if he had to. His other home, the one he had shared with Kate, hadn't that already disappeared into the maw of the anti-Catholic monster? By what right did this monster steal your nation from its faith, steal the money from your purse, the roof over your head and the clothes off your back for doing no more than seeking to worship God in the way of your fathers? By what right!

He calmed himself and slowed his horse for a second time. Possessions did not matter to him any more, he decided. He was ... *inflamed* by God. He was ready for the martyr's sacrifice to achieve the sacred end.

His mind turned back to practicalities. The squadrons of horses needed to carry revolution around the country once Parliament was annihilated? John Grant of Stratford could be counted on to provide some of them. Grant was a good man, solid, reliable, not given to talk. Both of them had been mixed up in the rebellion led by the Earls of Essex and Southampton in the time of the old Queen. Both had survived, at a cost of money not blood.

Who else?

Nearer the time, *nearer the time*, he told himself. The names would be found. It would all come together nearer the time.

The plans for the monarchy after James's damnation and the ripping out of the heretic weed from English soil? The infant Princess Elizabeth, young, malleable, disposable to the right Catholic husband in time, she lived in the Midlands within striking distance of John Grant's team. Yes, she would be promised in marriage to a good Catholic prince. All the same, there would need to be an interim leader, one chosen from the Catholic nobility, one who must survive the blast to take a new Government forward.

There was one he had in mind.

It awed him to think how much could be achieved by a determined few. Not too many in the know, *that* was the single lesson from all the failures before including the Essex fiasco, the lesson he constantly repeated to the hastier men he had recruited to the cause.

'Christ relied on twelve, we shall be no more.'

Garnet's safehouse came into view. He *must* overcome the Jesuit's prevarications. He could not allow the Jesuit to play for time. Time was not on their side.

Time was telling them it must be *now*.

Palmer had not been inside the Mermaid tavern in years.

With the fear of disease and the exodus from London, he found it sparsely populated. It made the landlord happy to see a stranger.

'I've not seen you in here before,' the man said.

Palmer shook his hand without giving a name.

'Business bring you to London, Mr er...?' William Johnson the landlord asked.

He was a bookseller from Canterbury, Palmer said, giving no name.

'We have a regular book-loving crowd here, you know.'

Palmer managed a look of innocent surprise.

'... the moving spirit is Mr Jonson the, ah, *classical* author. No relation!'

A man to stand on his dignity, Palmer guessed on hearing the doubtless self-description. He continued to play the impressionable provincial, asking who else belonged to this circle.

'There's Mr Shakespeare, but he would be the first to say that Mr Jonson, Ben, that is,' the landlord confided, implying that they were bosom friends, 'Ben is the life and soul. The younger sorts gravitate to him.'

Palmer took his chance.

'I should be privileged to meet Mr Jonson, I might be able to sell his works – we have a very discerning readership in Canterbury.'

The landlord appeared reluctant.

'.... and pay tribute to his genius in beer?' Palmer suggested.

The landlord was not yet persuaded.

'.... and dinner of course, for the two of us,' Palmer added, damned if he was going to pay for all the hangers-on as well.

'I *think* our man is still in town,' Johnson said, 'but I can't be certain sure. He's heavily occupied in an entertainment, a collaboration with Mr Inigo Jones – the, ah, master of design, do you know of him? No?'

Palmer shook his head.

'Just the same, tonight is a regular one for Ben if he is around.'

Pretty well every night was, Palmer guessed.

'Perhaps come back later, after seven? I would be happy to introduce you then. If Ben can be persuaded – a private dinner perhaps, something light, not more than half a dozen plates, oh, and wine, we have excellent French wines. Mr Jonson does have a taste for the *best* we have....'

'No, no, no!'

Catesby was adamant. Garnet tackled him again.

'I am not asking you to take my word or to accept my guidance alone, but you must consider what I have now heard from Rome.'

Garnet brandished a letter. Catesby waved the dangerous document aside. Putting things in writing – had no-one learned?

Garnet persisted.

'It insists that you must inform our Holy Father of your scheme before you carry it out. There is no scope for individual action, Robin.'

Catesby had difficulty in suppressing his old anger. It was all so typical that when action was called for, men of words prevaricated. Well, the priests in the Temple were not going to block God's will this time if he had anything to do with it.

'If His Holiness knew what we are planning, he would welcome it!'

'That is for him to say. Robin, you know that I cannot break the seal of your confession. So it must be you who tells Rome what you intend to do'.

Catesby gave the Jesuit a withering look.

'That would be madness, it would be *asking* to be caught. Have we learned nothing from all the previous attempts? Involve as few people as possible, put nothing in writing ... and now you want to offer up a hostage to fortune by doing exactly that, putting it in writing, running the gauntlet of Salisbury's spies at home and abroad. I won't do it!'

'Then we must send a messenger.'

He gave a name, someone he knew Catesby would trust, a man of his own generation. Garnet had already decided to write to his own superior about general fears of violence against King James without breaking the sanctity of the confessional – Rome would be worried by that. Yes, refer the matter upwards, slow things down to allow a solution to present itself, please God.

Catesby bit back his first reaction, to oppose the proposal to send a messenger. A second voice told him differently, that such a man might be encouraged to start late and 'hurry slowly' as the ancients put it. He might use a delay in which he could act uncontradicted by Garnet, and unconfined.

'All right,' he agreed.

'So we send the messenger and wait for the reply,' Garnet confirmed.

'We send the messenger, yes,' said Catesby, choosing his words.

Palmer set himself to watch the comings and goings at the Mermaid in the early evening. At last he saw a short, burly man approach, a bruiser dressed in a plain black suit a cut above the common man's. It was Jonson, he reckoned

He followed him in at a distance, saw him spoken to by the landlord, scratch his head and then laugh, presumably at the promise of a free dinner. Palmer left it for a minute or two and then approached the pair of them.

'Ah, Mr er....!' the landlord greeted him, 'we were just talking about you.'

'Mr Henry,' Palmer said. 'William Henry.' It was one of a number of aliases he used.

Jonson was shorter, with a mop of unruly hair swept back from his forehead, the sort best described as being as broad as he was tall. He gripped Palmer strongly by the hand with a paw which Palmer could feel had wielded more than a pen in its time.

'I hear you are a bookseller from Canterbury. So what's selling at the moment among the country philistines?'

Palmer allowed himself a smile at the jibe.

'Not much in your line, we do better with works of religious commentary,' he said.

Jonson set himself foursquare, waiting to hear more.

'We still have a call for some of the older poets – Sidney, Spenser,' Palmer said, picking his way among the safely dead.

'Any call for our friend Shakespeare?' Jonson interrupted, just a hint of rivalry in his tone.

'Some. His Venus, his Lucrece....'

God knows, he'd never read them but he had reason to know the names.

'Yes, and I can see why,' Jonson smiled, 'but I'm not sure that the classical epic was ever Will's strength. Don't get me wrong, I worship the man – this side of idolatry – but his classical education is, let's be honest about it, *not* his strongest point. His Latin is, well, pedestrian, and as for his Greek....'

Palmer shared the joke with another pale smile.

'But let's not talk about *him*', Jonson said. 'What I really want to know is – what's the market for plays by us more up-to-date authors? My friends are always on at me to publish, but my work is mainly in the theatre or for the entertainments I am now engaged on at Court. You may have heard, I work with Mr Inigo Jones – no? – well, he sets what I write is the truth of it, very much the junior partner. Words first, I say! No words, no art, whatever Mr Jones might think! But to return to our shekels, I've never been convinced that there *is* a serious market for published plays and the like. Tom Thorpe *did* publish Sejanus for me – has it reached Canterbury? What do *you* think my market there might be?'

Palmer was saved by the return of the landlord announcing that their private room was ready. The call of food and drink in a private room he guessed would suppress Jonson's inquisitiveness, for the time being.

They found the table cluttered not only with pewterware but glass as well, warning Palmer of an expensive bill. Bread and a hot soup were already waiting. As they sat down to eat, Palmer saw familiar, ancient words of Grace form silently on Jonson's lips. He completed them himself out loud, words which had not passed his lips since his days in his father's house.

Jonson looked cautiously around him. There were no witnesses to report what had been said.

'You are taking a risk, Mr Henry. I could be an informer. Or maybe that's what you are?'

Palmer did his best to look shocked.

'After all, what would a provincial bookseller be doing in London in plague-time?' Jonson asked, ignoring the food for the moment.

'I get better prices from the publishers when their market's struggling,' Palmer replied, 'so my profits are bigger back in Canterbury.'

'Oh you ... *shopkeeper!*' Jonson roared.

His eyes were already wandering back to the food and drink. Palmer watched him tackle the soup, stopping only to swig deeply from his beer mug. Finally the writer took breath to speak again.

'I was not born into the faith,' he said in a voice softer than before, as if he was shedding a mask. 'There was a priest, when I spent some time in prison back in '98 – a slight misunderstanding with a fellow actor, the second man I killed; the other was in action, in Flanders.'

Old soldiers like Palmer rarely talked of killing. But there was no stopping the man opposite.

'My faith is no secret from the authorities, they suspect me of being a recusant, and it's true, I avoid their church services. I swear I'd even pay my fines *if* they caught up with me!'

He laughed out loud and, then, with a nod, passed the obligation of confession onto his partner.

To lie well it is best to stay close to the truth. Palmer gave him the story of his own father's slide through faith into poverty. That recusancy was a mug's game he was careful not to say.

'So your father was a gentleman', Jonson observed. 'Mine was too, a clergyman but he died before I was born – inconveniently for me. I was well educated though, by Camden – you know of him? Yes, of course you would, you're a man of books. At Westminster School as it happens, better educated than our friend Shakespeare in his country grammar, bless him. But my mother remarried – a bricklayer … nothing wrong with that, it's a lucrative trade. Trouble was,' and here Jonson leaned towards his host, 'he saw everything as it stood in relation to the building trade. He was a man for bricks and mortar rather than questions of the mind.'

Servants brought in salvers of beef and fowl. Jonson promptly helped himself, filling his mouth while at the same time continuing his story.

'He got me to follow him into the trade – I've done my time at it, I can tell you, I'm a first-class bricklayer, I keep up my membership of the guild. Many's the time it's put bread on the table when the theatre let me down, I can tell you. Anyway, where was I? Oh, yes, whenever the Government published some edict or other, my stepfather would ask "what does this mean for builders?" I wouldn't have minded if he had been generous to his scholar stepson. You see, I could have been a Cambridge man – well, I *was*, for a few weeks, until the money ran out.'

A Cambridge man himself, Palmer said nothing. Jonson ploughed on.

'Maybe my stepfather was right, maybe if people kept to their own business there would be less trouble in the world.'

Palmer saw his opportunity.

'Then men would abandon their consciences, as many have abandoned their faith.' It was true, about himself.

Had he gone too far? The pair fell silent until the next dishes were brought in. When the servants had gone, Jonson spoke softly again.

'That's our dilemma, to choose between the world of ideas or the practicalities of the world.'

He said no more on the subject. For the rest of the meal, both men kept the conversation within the bounds of polite exchange and masculine gossip. At the end, when Palmer stood up to find the landlord and settle the account, Jonson detained him with a hand on his sleeve.

'I hope we meet again when *I* shall return the hospitality, if you find me in funds, that is;' and he laughed, unashamed. 'I'd invite you to the little club we have here but the town is pretty much deserted. Maybe another time?'

Palmer bowed gracefully.

A late thought came to his guest.

'There are other friends, more of our *mind* whom you might like to meet.'

Palmer's ears pricked up.

'... gentlemen all, full of themselves as our so-called gentlemen are. I'll let you know – or you can always find me here at the Mermaid. Meantime I shall have business in Oxford where the Court is due. I am thankfully not called upon professionally, but,' said Jonson, grinning at his host, 'we parasites must be ready to feed upon our King and Master.'

'Will you be put up with the Court in Woodstock?' Palmer asked.

'Lord, no. We in the acting trade prefer our own. The Town Tavern is our favourite, it has a very handsome landlady.'

It was not late when Palmer left Jonson, his purse lighter than he had intended.

He made his way gradually in the direction of his Clerkenwell lodgings. At the Bell in Carter Lane he put in his first appearance in a week. The look on the landlord's face showed that it was a double bonus – to reclaim a customer and have his slate paid off at the same time.

Restless, Palmer had one tankard of beer and then went on his way. He toyed with the idea of paying for a woman for the night but he lacked the desire. The residual wheeze in his lungs was making him conscious of his own mortality. He decided not to tempt a Fate he had come to believe in as much as he didn't in a God.

He could feel that the nights were closing in again. They brought a hint of cold, the presentiment of autumn with winter to follow. Palmer was comforted by the money in his purse, despite its depletion by the supper with Jonson.

He entered his tenement in Cowcross Street, making his way up to his chamber. Was the smell of the place always this vile? He could not be bothered to throw a light on the squalor. He undressed in the dark. The bed welcomed him with the sanctity of clean sheets. It was his one sanctuary in an otherwise maculate existence. He drifted off into a sleep purchased by the cost of a nightmare, of fighting and survival at any cost.

~ 4 ~

UGUST into September was a time of travel.

For Robin Catesby he had his Stratford house to sell to raise more money for the cause. Father Garnet was planning a pilgrimage, to a shrine in Wales – it was an act of prudence to get out of Catesby's way. Guido Fawkes slipped back into London from the continent where he had been sent to avoid the risk of random discovery.

Richard Palmer stayed put in London. He paid a visit to Salisbury in Whitehall to obtain orders. The Chief Minister pointed his investigator in a fresh direction.

'Keep an eye out for any Percys you come across – I have little faith in their chief, Lord Northumberland. Nevertheless your priority remains the Jesuit, Garnet – he is slippery, he has been on the run for nearly twenty years. Whatever is going on – and I remain certain that something is – Garnet will be at the centre of it. The time is coming for you to move in closer.'

'I'd like to have a list of those implicated in earlier troubles,' Palmer requested, referring to plots Salisbury had already crushed.

Salisbury waved agreement without discussion, his attention shifting to other duties. When he looked up again, he saw that Palmer was still there.

'Well?' he asked.

'Why has Garnet never been picked up before?'

Salisbury was tempted to give him the official line. Instead he chose the truth.

'He has been lucky, our pursuers have been close to him several times. I'd rather have had him in the bag, but if not, then better the devil you know than one you do not. The man is no St. Paul. We have always found him, let us say, manageable. There has been an argument that to root him out him would have meant Rome replacing the loss, and that might have entailed someone...'

'More valiant for the cause?'

'Just so. We have had Garnet roughly where we wanted him, and it has been useful to have a single figure of fear for public contemplation, especially when we knew that he was no great threat. This is no longer the case, however.'

'So what has changed?'

'Hard to put one's finger on it. There is a new Pope in Rome, so will the policy of 'beat the drum but do nothing' persist? At the same time, our intelligence is reporting movement among the activists. What if Garnet has lost control over the harder men? That is my instinct, and my fear.'

'You're asking a lot of someone in my position....' Palmer began to say.

Salisbury looked up abruptly.

'And what position would that be?'

'There are no pensions for the free-lance.' No perks for weighing hay, Palmer was thinking, of Lanier, as he spoke.

Salisbury shook his head tolerantly.

'Pick up an extra purse from my official when you ask him for the list you want. Failing all else, meet me at Oxford towards the end of the month.'

Oxford? Just where Jonson had said he was going.

It took Palmer time and a lot of clerical clicking of tongues to procure the required information from the files.

The first chance Palmer had to look at it was over a tankard of beer in the Bell Inn. Of the names he read, many had prospered as favoured men in the new regime of King James. Take for example Lord Monteagle. He was Catholic and a recusant who had escaped with a huge fine for his part in an earlier coup, the Essex uprising. He was 'toeing the line' according to the file which also recorded that he had not, as yet, paid the fine in full.

The name of Thomas Percy also stood out, after Salisbury's tip about the family – another previous malcontent now 'living in lodgings next to Parliament in order to fulfil his duties as a bodyguard of the King.' Another one on the gravy train, Palmer reckoned. The name of Robin Catesby did not detain him long, an unimportant one on the face of it, way down the list in the Essex affair.

Swilling the beer around his mouth, Palmer reckoned that August would be a dead month. He debated how to use the time – by going up to Oxford early? Or keeping an eye on Ben Jonson at the Mermaid? One or the other, it felt very, very good compared to his position just a week before.

Palmer found Jonson friendly when he caught up with him a few days later in Bread Street.

'It never ceases to amaze me,' Jonson growled, 'how difficult it is to raise money for art. You see all sorts picking up backhanders just because of how they were born, who they married or who they know – and don't talk to *me* about marriage, I've had enough of it, of women too for that matter. Now, I happen to be after our noble Lord – Salisbury I mean – and you'd think I was asking for the Crown jewels. What does he do? He keeps me dangling while other arselickers slip in and out, crawling up his fundament to get their nice little earners. No,' Jonson announced without bothering to keep his voice down, 'Salisbury's not one to help you a minute longer than you're useful to him.'

The irony that it was Salisbury's money paying while Jonson was venting his spleen against him, almost amused Palmer.

'Perhaps our *affiliations* have something to do with it?' he speculated, leading Jonson on.

'I dare say, but there again, I know men of our faith who have done well, men of rank admittedly, as I was saying before....'

Palmer held his tongue and waited. His patience was rewarded.

'There's Lord Mordaunt, Monteagle of course, and plenty of others who have conveniently inveigled themselves into the new order. Wasn't always so, I can tell you.'

Only the first name was new to Palmer.

'Then there are others who haven't needed it,' Jonson went on. 'Frank Tresham, now, he's just inherited a fortune after the death of his father who was a veritable tyrant for our faith – *there's* a thought, I should go after Frank for money....'

'But there must be others who, like us,' Palmer dwelled on the last two words, 'haven't done so well?'

'Yes, yes, that's true, one must count one's blessings as my old mum says.'

A silence fell between them. Palmer knew he must not speak, even if Jonson's mug was getting dangerously empty. A call for more beer and the train of revelation might be broken. Jonson was tapping the mug on the table in irritation. Palmer waited for the next words.Come on Jonson...

'Take Robin Catesby for example,' Jonson said.

Palmer's interest deflated. A bit player from what he recollected on the file, also mixed up in the Essex uprising but not one of the big fish the Chief Minister was interested in.

'... a man of parts if ever there was one, but he got himself into trouble – lost half his land as a result in order to pay the fines, and there are rumours he's selling the rest of what he has in Stratford.'

Palmer called for more beer.

'Very generous of you, Mr Henry,' Jonson said. 'Wish I could return it, but times is 'ard.'

The joke appeared to set the playwright thinking.

'Some of my finer friends are better placed in the matter of shekels. After what I've just said about Catesby, I should feel bad about accepting hospitality from him, but he's to give a private dinner in the autumn when everyone is back, very *select.*'

Jonson played on the word with a roguish grin.

'Robin likes to be a man about the town when he's not busy rushing all over the country. Would you like to be invited as my guest? It might repay the hospitality you've given me.'

Palmer nodded. Bit players could often lead you to the main men, the men Salisbury was interested in, like the Percys and their ilk.

Palmer made a point of depositing a report in Whitehall to be put in front of the Chief Minister before he left for Oxford. It never harmed to keep the information ticking up in front of the client. It reassured them that you were on the job, their job.

To travel to Oxford he hired a horse. It was time for a little holiday, he decided and Jonson had told him that he would be there for the visit of the Court. In following him up, Palmer intended to find out more about who he was mixing with – you were never more than a step or two from your target; the skill lay in making the connections, was his experience.

The weather was mixed as the travelling party rode out on the Oxford road. The air was oppressive, the summer heat throwing a stifling haze over the landscape, veiling the sun. It was the ripening rather than the growing time. Was it also the incubating time for conspiracy, if Salisbury was to be believed?

Palmer thought about the minor players in the Essex affair, men like who was it? Catesby, the one Jonson said was selling up. What did their sort do next, once they were displaced in their own country? Go to the wars in Flanders? Not any more, mercenary work was far less regular these days after peace with Spain and Catesby was a fighting man if Jonson was to be believed, a landless one too, forced to make a change, to what? He would be restless, dissatisfied, an obvious candidate to be drawn into political discontent by some mastermind ... such as Garnet the Jesuit. And who else? Spiritual power always needed the assistance of the temporal, the hands clasped in prayer held up by a strong right arm.

It was the better part of a two day ride to Oxford when taken at an easy pace, which suited Palmer and his out-of-practice rump. He lodged at a small inn in preference to the Town Tavern recommended by Jonson. He preferred to see him at his own time of choosing.

The Cambridge man in Palmer could not help making comparisons with the rival university town. The first difference he noticed was the absence of wind. Cambridge and wind, alternately biting or nagging in winter, unseasonal in summer, formed an unbreakable marriage. Cambridge lay open to the east and the cold North Sea. Oxford in the Midlands took weather from every direction or none at all.

Oxford had the bustle and variety of a city. Town was as important as gown in contrast to its East Anglian younger sister where gown predominated. Trade routes from all points of the compass travelled through its midland location. Government had left its mark at different times and continued to do so. Oxford was a polis, Cambridge a village. It made sense that the Court came to stay near Oxford and never to the other place.

Palmer wandered down the Broad to view the city's grandest avenue. He admired two great colleges brushed with the patina of age, of three or four centuries at least. When he wandered south, a much newer one, the sin of Cardinal Wolsey's pride looked barely marked in comparison; and alongside it evidence of plenty of new, yellow stone shaping fresh accommodation for the growing population of the city.

Coming back into the centre, he happened on the Town Tavern without looking for it.

The landlord was not the jovial sort, Palmer discovered as they exchanged greetings when he went in, not like William Johnson at the Mermaid. Conviviality was not part of the welcome John Davenant offered beyond a basic politeness to new custom. It was the landlady who came out to ask if he wanted to eat.

Palmer found Jane Davenant everything her husband was not. She was darkly pretty, with a skill in conversation beyond the knack of chat. As Mrs Davenant passed his order to a serving girl, she turned back to talk to the new face in the room, Palmer's. She had grey eyes. Palmer liked fine eyes in a woman. There had been one whose eyes were dark...

To her first question, he admitted that he had come from London.

'I promise that I won't ask your business,' she laughed, a pleasant low sound, excellent in woman. 'but what does London offer at this time of year, with the Court out of town?'

Not a lot, Palmer was happy to concede, especially with plague restrictions still in force.

'...which means the playhouses will be closed as well,' the landlady was quick to point out, explaining how she and her husband were Londoners in origin.

Oh how women loved the plays ... and the players, Palmer reminded himself.

'Business is good for us when the acting companies come here,' she explained, 'and there is talk that they may come up for the visit of Their Majesties to the University.'

'Yes, so I hear.' Palmer's reply lacked enthusiasm.

'You are not a man for the drama,' she challenged him.

Palmer was not. He found it childish and ignorant of the classical principles necessary to make any attempt at composition worthwhile. Where was their unity of time, manner and place? All over the place from what he had seen, what with events spread over days and years in a host of different locations, in different countries even! Holding the mirror up to nature indeed! He only ever went to the plays under protest and on business, usually to track straying wives.

If the woman opposite liked the plays, was *she* straight, he wondered, or one of the sort who offered something on the side? Plenty of inns added bedmate to board and lodge.

'Nor is my husband,' he heard Mrs Davenant say, 'fond of the playhouse, though he does approve of Mr Shakespeare. I doubt you've heard of him....'

Palmer was brought mentally upright at the name. The last time he had been in Oxford was in pursuit of the very man.

'It is a name I have heard,' he allowed himself to say, as casual as you like.

'He's an actor, a King's Man, Mr er...'

'Henry,' Palmer lied.

'Mr Shakespeare stays with us on his way to and from London. He comes from Stratford, where he has property.'

Palmer had seen it, and what could be bought in the country with London profits.

'John, my husband, is going to ask him to stand godfather to our child … if it's a boy.'

So the woman was with child, by her husband it was to be hoped.

'When is the … er ….' Palmer asked.

Mrs Davenant beamed with pleasure.

'Late February or early March. Now, do you already have accommodation in the city, Mr Henry?'

Palmer said that he had, and where.

'It's a clean house,' she conceded as she was getting up to leave him, to eat in peace. 'But if you should ever be tempted to change then we would be happy to welcome you here.'

Palmer thanked her, appreciating what the dour Mr Davenant had in his wife.

'Tell me, when do you expect the Court here in Oxford?' he asked her.

'In three or four days.'

'So you will be busy here at the inn?'

'Full to bursting.'

'Including the actors?'

'We believe so.'

'Well, good luck to you,' Palmer said.

When she took it as a reference to her condition, he looked away, embarrassed.

The days of waiting were lucky with the weather. Palmer saw more sights of the city. On the third day he walked out east, beyond a deer park, across open fields alongside a confluence of rivers.

He found himself at a bend in the flow in a secluded spot. The freshness of the water against the heat of the day tempted him. There was no-one around. Stripping down and slipping into the welcoming cold water, he saw where his white skin was marked by the recent infection. He had been a swimmer in his youth. Was that the last time? No, it was on campaign, he reminded himself, in a cold river in the Low Countries, to wash away the stains of war.

He let himself wallow in the water. When the cold began to creep into muscle and bone, he struck out into the middle of the river, over to the other side.

It was the sound of a deeper splash from elsewhere which stopped him in mid stroke. The sound was eerie, like the determined plop of a beast launching itself into the stream with unfriendly intent. There was no voice, no shout. Palmer tensed, imagining childish things. He trod water, before pushing himself in the direction of the original noise.

At first there was nothing to be seen. He reached up to an overhanging branch from a riverside tree and pulled himself halfway out of the water.

He saw what he was looking for.

It was a human form, face down and sinking, dragged down by a woman's skirts. Was she dead? Who had pushed her in? Palmer scanned the bank. There was no-one to be seen.

The body began jerking intermittently. Palmer threw himself forward from the bough and swam towards the cargo in the water. He called out – no answer, no movement. He hesitated for a moment then, as the body began to disappear, he ducked under the water. His aim was to force the body upwards. It did not resist. As it came to the surface, he pulled the head up and turned the body round.

He saw the face of a young woman, eyes closed but mouth still breathing. He felt for the river bottom with his feet, unsuccessfully which told him that they were both out of their depth. He turned over onto his back and cradled her on his chest as he manoeuvred towards the far bank.

Getting the girl out of the water was the hardest part. Palmer stood up to find himself in shallow water, trying to find a purchase on the riverbed. He felt himself sucked into spongy, sticky mud up to his calves. He was close to exhaustion. He was not the athlete of his youth and the depredations of the recent illness were rapidly weakening him.

The girl was coming round into sluggish consciousness.

'Can you hear me?' Palmer gasped, struggling to support her. She gave a low moan. He tried again with his question.

'Yaas,' she succeeded in saying, in one word, the accent of a country girl.

Palmer examined the bank. Branches and scrub close to hand might get them out if she could help. He told her what to do.

'Grab hold of this,' he gasped again, pulling a branch down. He saw her hand take hold, without much grip. His patience was fading with his bodily strength, 'For Christ's sake, hold onto it!' He saw her fingers respond, encouraging each other, one by one, to grip the wood.

'Now the other hand!'

Palmer watched as the second hand repeated the action of the first.

'Now, when I shove, pull yourself up as much as you can.'

At the third attempt he felt her body shift and force itself onto the bank. There it lay motionless. Palmer heaved himself out before realising that save for his drawers, he was naked. It couldn't be helped, he had no strength left to swim to the other side where his clothes were. He was grateful for the beating rays of the sun which began to penetrate his aching limbs.

He forced the body of the girl onto her side. She coughed then vomited water. She was shivering despite the summer heat, breathing with difficulty . Palmer loosened the strings of her bodice before unlacing them, pushing the garment away. Next he began to pull her waterlogged skirt down. He heard mumbled protests and felt feeble physical resistance.

'It's not what you think,' he said as he dragged the heavy clothing free and spread it under the full glare of the midday sun.

The girl was left in her shift. With a painful effort, she raised herself into a sitting position, shivering all the while, cradling her knees in her arms. Then she raised her haunches and slipped her shift over her head.

It was then that Palmer saw the outline of the child in her belly.

'I slipped an' fell in.'

They were her first sensible words to him and they were nonsense. If it was an accident she would have cried out, struggled, splashed around. Palmer could see that she was young, sixteen or seventeen, her hair, drying fast in the sun alongside her clothes, fading into a pale red colour. She seemed careless of the man's near-nakedness next to her.

'We'd be better in the shade,' Palmer said, feeling warmth turn to burning on his shoulders.

'Oh yaas,' she mocked. The old, old story, was it?

'Well, that's where I'm going,' he said, standing up and striding off into the nearby shade.

When he got there, he looked up and down the river. There was no crossing. He would have to swim to the other side to pick up his clothes. He had saved her once. If she tried to kill herself again, then that was up to her. He began to worry more about the purse of money which sat inside his clothes on the other bank, beyond his power to protect it.

Just as he made up his mind to start back into the water, the girl heaved herself up and began walking over towards him. She was a primitive Eve, like an altarpiece he had seen in a church on campaign abroad, skin white and translucent under the dazzle of the bright sun. He noticed the delicate tracery of blue veins tracking through her body. She carry-cradled the bulge in front of her as she walked. She was not large, it was as if her normal, slender body had not been designed to support the incubus within her. Palmer was shocked to see from her skinny limbs and extruding ribs that she was underfed.

She sank to her knees in front of him, saying nothing. Palmer's worry for his money returned. He hesitated over what to do.

'When is the baby due?' he asked.

The girl shook her head slowly.

'A month, maybe less, don' rightly know.'

'What is your name?'

'Ellen,' she replied, answering his catechising.

Ellen, Helen, it was a name he liked – he had never known a bad one. His godmother had been a Helen, dead inevitably, gone like everything in the past.

'And your family name?'

'Got no other name, got no parents, leastwise, not livin' I 'aven't.'

'Got a husband or a man?' Palmer asked.

She shook her head.

'Where do you live?' he asked, an eye and most of his mind on the other bank.

She gave him the name of an inn which he did not know, where she worked, she said, as a servant. She had walked out from town to where they were now. There had obviously been a crisis, Palmer realised, because it was a weekday and the only holiday for a serving girl would be a Sunday half day.

'What happened?'

'Mistress found out.'

'And threw you out?'

'Stands to reason once she found out.... I 'ad to tell 'er the baby was the master's.... I tried to 'ide it, near starved us both to death, but it wouldn't stop growin'.'

There was nothing Palmer could say.

'Didn't want to.... not with the master. I told 'im the mistress would be angry if I did. 'E said 'e'd be angry if I didn't, so you take your pick missy, 'e said.'

Palmer stopped himself from speaking. He had saved her, wasn't that enough? Maybe it would have been kinder to leave her in the water. He could her give her a little money, if he got back to the other side, to his money and his clothes.

'Ain't got nowhere to go,' she said, answering the unasked question.

The answer lay with the Church, with a priest who would know what to do. The priest would pass her onto the parish for lodging, work and poor relief. Palmer said as much to her.

'I ain't goin' on the parish.' Her child's face set stubbornly. 'Ra-ather go back in the water.'

Palmer made an excuse – he needed to go back over to the other side for his clothes. From there he could leg it. He had done enough already, the rest was up to her.

'You want a bit?' she offered sullenly, rubbing between her legs, anxious to keep hold of her rescuer. 'I can still do it, I was still doin' it with the master.'

It did not attract him. Without another word, he slid back down into the river, felt it sharply cold against his overheated skin and swam towards the other side. He clambered out without looking back. His clothes were still there and the purse too. Yes, he would leave without looking back. He had done enough, maybe too much....

It was then that he heard her scream.

5

THE SCREAM repeated itself and became a series of howls, each one more frenzied than the last. There was a pause, before four words hurtled over the water between them.

'Sweet Jesus ... the baby!'

The howling continued, strange, animal, not the cries of normal female distress – he was familiar enough with those – but ululations of some deep, primeval pain. Unwillingly, he turned round. The girl was writhing on the ground. Don't go back, *don't* go back his mind lectured him, but when he moved it was to fold up his clothes and swim across the river on his back, holding the bundle above the water as best he could.

He had no idea what to do – birth was woman's stuff, women with women in a secluded chamber and for the men, hours of waiting, if they bothered to be there at all. He had seen all sorts of horrors in battle, the slip and slither of human offal, and the stench, but he was unprepared for childbirth.

There was liquid between the girl's legs.

''S all right,' she reassured him, 'me waters broke, and the baby....'

She grimaced as regular shocks of pain from bodily contractions surged through her.

'... the baby's comin' ... comin' quickly.'

Palmer knelt down beside her. All he could think of was the need to make her comfortable. She preferred to rest on her back with her head and shoulders raised and supported on her elbows. He stuffed the parcel of his clothes behind her, collecting hers in order to double the cushion.

She held out a hand to grip his forearm as if to steady herself, locking onto it every time a spasm of pain came. Her grip was like a dying man's, like an enemy soldier Palmer remembered, a Spaniard who had clung to him, his eyes rigid in their demand that he stay with him as he approached death. He felt her nails bite into his flesh with increasing frequency. There was a rhythm in this, he guessed, trying to help her into it. He used soothing words, words last heard when his mother used to nurse him in infancy.

Some awful climax appeared to be approaching by the way she was arching her back while pushing, grunting and screaming. Her heels fought to gain purchase on the ground, she thrust her knees as wide as she could shouting at him to help her keep them open. He leaned forward to place his palms like dividers, pushing outwards at the top of her scrawny thighs.

'Hwa!' The sound was like one mighty last effort, followed by another one. To Palmer's amazement, the head of a baby began to appear from between her legs.

'Keep pushing,' he shouted.

'Help it,' she gasped.

He had no idea how but something told him that pulling it out like a newborn lamb was not the best course of action. He scrambled down the side of her body so that he could put his hands under the emerging foetus.

And then it came, in a slurry of blood and mucus and, to his astonishment, attached by a long cord. The mother gave a last gasp of relief before sinking back into a prone position. Her breathing, accompanied by the movement of her ribcage was stertorous.

In his hands, Palmer held a tiny little girl.

But she wasn't moving ... and there was no breathing.... Christ, all that effort, and now this ... or did it matter? Maybe it was for the best.

'Cut the cord,' the mother demanded.

There was still no sign of life. Palmer scrambled back up to where his clothes were, pulling out the knife he kept in one of his boots in a special leather sleeve. He went back and performed the operation, pulling the tiny body free.

'It was a girl,' he announced sombrely.

She heard the omen in his voice.

'What's the matter?' she demanded, in the anxious voice of a mother who moments before was just a child. She struggled up into a half raised position. 'Oh no! Sweet Jesus....'

'What do I do?' Palmer asked.

'Slap its arse!'

'Slap its arse? How hard?'

'Just slap it !'

Palmer did as he was told. The baby remained inert. He heard the mother begin to sob, then keen with a scream of miserable grief like no other sound he had heard on earth.

'Give me my baby!' she moaned at last.

'Not like this,' Palmer said, getting up to take the little corpse off to the river.

The river was where he would wash her. Then he would bury her so that she couldn't be found, otherwise who could be sure there wouldn't be a charge of infanticide brought against him and the girl? He sat at the water's edge, ready to dunk the tiny body in the cold water, once to clean the mess off her body and a second time as a kind of oblation. The body was still warm. He thrust it in, under and out once more, turning his head away to check on the mother who was watching him, silently, like a cautious wild animal.

He thought at first he must be imagining the light sensation in his hands. Before his eyes could check, his ears heard the sound, a thin, high mewling, spluttering sound and he felt the little package vibrating in his hands.

'It's alive!' he shouted. 'It's a bloody miracle!'

They wrapped the infant in cloth ripped from the skirt of the girl's shift. The mother was sore, but being young there appeared to be little further bleeding, not once the rest of the birth matter was out. They rested a couple of hours, in the shade, the baby clutched into the mother's breast.

'Do you think you can walk?' Palmer asked.

'Goin' to have to,' was all she said, 'but I ain't goin' on the parish, so if that's your idea, you can leave us 'ere. We'll shift for usselves.'

The walk back into the city was slow, Palmer supporting the mother, the mother cradling the baby for dear life.

Palmer's first tactic was to consult the couple at the inn where he was lodging, an old childless pair by all accounts. Perhaps if they took a fancy to the girl and her offspring, they might take her in? The look of disbelief on their faces at his tale of finding the girl and child in the country soon disabused him. They insisted that he find accommodation elsewhere.

'It's a respectable house we're used to keeping!' the landlord said, backed up by his wife.

Palmer's temper flared.

'You're a pair of sanctimonious old miseries! Now, while I pick up my belongings, you bring my horse round....'

'You're not going without paying your bill.'

'Pay the bill?'

Palmer threatened them with the authorities. It had the desired effect. They knew enough to realise that you could never be sure about a stranger, who he was, who he knew; and this one said he was working for the Chief Minister!

Palmer lifted the mother side-saddle onto a horse, passing the newborn up to her. He took the leading reins and walked the little group on. They went in the direction of the Town Tavern.

He made sure that he spoke to the landlady first and in private.

'It was an act of Christian charity,' Jane Davenant declared, conscious of her own child within her.

Palmer was taken aback. To him it was neither, he'd had little choice in the matter. When he told her the girl's story, where she had come from, who she claimed the father was, Mrs Davenant's mouth tightened and her grey eyes flashed.

'My husband will speak to him, I'll make sure of that. The child will be supported by the father unless he wants to be called in by the bawdy court for lewd behaviour ... and if the girl's honest, we can always find room for another maidservant ... when she's recovered from the birth.'

There remained the matter of Palmer's own accommodation. Mrs Davenant repeated her offer.

'I expect you will be busy with the actors of the King's Men,' he said.

'We've had word from them,' Jane Davenant told him. 'They are not now required by the Court, so they aren't coming.'

6

THE ARRIVAL of the Court transformed Oxford into a festival city, of the watchers and the watched.

A Court procession came in from the royal palace at Woodstock a few miles outside the city. Through the north gate monarch, courtiers and hangers-on swaggered into the city in front of a large crowd out to cheer them on in holiday mood. To Palmer's eye, they looked like a crowd of travelling players.

They halted to hear an erudite play of welcome in Latin, for which Palmer had found a close vantage point.

'See there – those are the three Sybils, prophetesses of ancient Rome,' he explained to the Davenants.

'Salve!'

A single figure stepped forward from among them, echoed by each of the others in a trio of salutations.

'Means "All hail",' Palmer whispered.

Latin verse rolled out from the mouths of the three student actors, young men for whom this would always be the day they performed before the King. Their voices were confident, and far too young. The verse singled out a name which Palmer couldn't quite catch, of an ancient ancestor of King James with the prophecy that his heirs would reign in Scotland, and then, the speaker claimed, in a *united* Britain.

A smattering of applause from the few who understood the Latin greeted the statement. Palmer recognised it as the political message it was – the union of Scotland and England, dear to the King's heart. Strange name, he thought, the one given to the ancestor. Had he got it right? Bankwo? Fair enough – who knew what weird and wonderful language the ancient

Scots spoke or the names they bore in consequence? Ben Jonson might, or his teacher Camden. Where *was* Jonson, Palmer wondered?

King James was trying to look pleased, Palmer could see. He had never seen the King close to before. He stood above middle height, his hair and beard reddish, well trimmed and restricted to the mask of the face, a face which responded to the attention of onlookers as an actor's might – a nod here and a smile there, above all a determination to show an easy command. But the forehead was furrowed, the eyes hooded while the mouth, which the King regularly brushed with the back of his sleeve in an uncouth manner, appeared to work hard to contain his tongue. He did not appear comfortable. His eyes were unsettled, unable to concentrate. People said he had a morbid fear of assassination, a fear born out of attempts on his life in Scotland.

Queen Anne at his side was the more adept, showing the public her enjoyment of what was going on. It was a new response, Palmer thought, pretending to like what you didn't. The royal child Henry presented an amalgam of the better parts of each parent. He carried himself with an attractive confidence for a youth approaching twelve.

'He will make a fine king when his time comes,' Mrs Davenant said.

'God willing,' was her husband's laconical response.

They were about to return to the tavern when a voice called out.

'Mr Palmer!'

It was Cecil's official.

Palmer strode away, ignoring the call so foolishly made when he was on business. Surely the man knew better? The Davenants did not appear to have noticed.

When they all got back to the tavern, news was given to John Davenant that Ben Jonson had arrived.

Why, Palmer wondered, if the plays and players were not required? He went to find him.

'Bless me, but it's Mr Henry!' Ben Jonson called out across the busy room, tapping his empty tankard in blatant suggestion.

Palmer ordered up a refill as well as one for himself.

'Have you seen any of the festivities?' Palmer asked.

'The Latin play, you mean? Unless it's one of mine, I try to avoid them as much as possible. As it is, I am making myself scarce away from London – the small matter of an unlicensed performance of my latest *wark*,' he said with a laugh. 'Got up the nose of the Scotch because of some uncomplimentary Caledonian references.'

So Jonson was not welcome for the time being in the capital. As William Henry the bookseller would, Palmer told Jonson more about the work he had just seen. Jonson remained unimpressed.

'Oh, God, yes, I've heard about it, written by one of your men of parts, doctor of medicine by day and verse doctor by night,' he said in a stage aside which could be heard by anyone who cared to listen. 'It surely sent the King to sleep,' he whispered more quietly. 'He only pretends to like the plays but the truth is, if it doesn't have four legs and feathers or fur, for the hunting thereof, then His Majesty is not really interested. It's Queen Anne who's keen. We do have high hopes of their boy, however.'

Jonson took a long draught of his beer then examined the inside of his mug as if the contents had been stolen. Palmer pretended not to notice. Jonson shrugged.

'No, I don't go in for academic sycophancies. I have a better line, you see, in these Court masques I was telling you about in London. I have another one lined up for Christmas, m'boy, good money too, though it means working with that bloody arselicker Jones, Inigo of that ilk, my so-called collaborator who says that masques are all about the paintin' and carpenterin' if you please. All the same,' he said, 'I must keep my hand in with the public stage. So I've been putting into Salisbury's mind the idea that something suitably *laudatory*, you know, boosting the Stuart name, could be a fit subject. He does seem receptive to the idea. I mean, the actors would pay me for my work on delivery but then, a sweetener from the Chief Minister in advance would make it all so much more worthwhile.'

Jonson consulted the tavern air for inspiration.

'What I need is a dramatic theme, one which plays well for today rather than some obscure episode in Scots history like the one you've just told me about. I am not fond of our Caledonian friends as you probably gathered. Must be the bricklayer in me.'

'I see, so you want to repair that impression,' Palmer said.

'Yes, but only up to a point. I am nobody's lapdog, as you can tell, but,' and here Jonson lowered his voice still further, 'we of the faith, you and I, we have to work harder in maintaining our credit with the powers-that-be.'

'Let's take a room where we can talk more privately,' Palmer said.

'No, I am no fanatic either,' Jonson assured Palmer once they were settled in and had food and drink in front of them, 'at least, not on the subject of religion.'

He relaxed in his chair in contemplation of a major assault on the food.

'It seems to me,' he said through a mouthful of beef, 'that a man should be able to practise his beliefs according to his conscience, which by and large the authorities let us Catholics do. Since I have no desire for public office, not yet awhile anyway, then it's all the same to me – I haven't been hindered from practising my craft after all; well, apart from a short stay at His Majesty's pleasure over the odd play, but that's a hazard of the job.'

'I'm relieved to hear it.' Palmer made to sound like the respectable bookseller from Kent. 'My father sailed closer to the wind', which was true, 'which did him and our family no good at all. One hears terrible talk these days, about threat of revolution and suchlike....'

Jonson put a reassuring hand on the investigator's arm.

'My kingdom is not of this world,' he quoted from scripture.

'That's as may be,' Palmer said, 'but I am anxious to stay clear of trouble in the present world.'

'Yes, I can understand that,' Jonson said, 'I can be too trusting myself. Being in the theatre is double-edged. On the one hand we are treated as a hotbed of sedition, on the other, when it comes down to it, we are not taken seriously. It is as if we are children, and that we don't live in the real world.'

He cut himself more meat.

'I *can* see that respectable folk such as you have to be extra cautious,' he conceded. 'So let us consider. That dinner I mentioned to you – when the invitation comes – Robin Catesby, well yes, he has a chequered past, but then so have a dozen others I could reel off who fell foul in the old world and have prospered in the new.'

'What is his background?' Palmer asked.

'The family has always been staunch in the faith, his father – died only a few years ago- he had his own troubles with the Government which cost him a lot of money and a spell inside ... and so Robin takes after him. That's why he was locked up at the end of Elizabeth's time.'

Palmer raised a disbelieving laugh.

'Apart from which he is a model citizen!'

Jonson shooed the implication aside.

'Other times, other customs. As I said, there's plenty with similar records and worse who are no risk to the state – Monteagle, for example. He was a ringleader in the Essex business when Robin was only a camp follower.'

'Was he now?' Palmer asked, and regretted it.

A silence fell over the room. Jonson's attitude cooled with it.

'Dangerous talk, Mr Henry.'

Palmer began to cover his tracks. 'I agree, and I mean nothing by it. In my circle, many are unhappy that promises in respect of the acceptance of our religion are not being kept. I distance myself from such people, because their concerns may be mistaken for thoughts and thoughts for intentions which are then claimed to be acts by the legal ferrets of the State.'

'I am not forcing you to accept anyone's hospitality, Mr Henry, you don't have to meet Catesby and his friends if you don't like....'

'Mr Jonson, I realise that I must appear a cautious soul, but even as I trust you – if I might be so bold – I must take each person as I find.'

'I'll drink to that,' Jonson retorted, indicating another empty mug.

'A child must have godparents, Mr Henry. It seems it was you brought the child into the world so there is no-one else who should have the honour before you.'

'And the responsibility, Mrs Davenant,' Palmer replied, caught off-guard by the suggestion from his landlady. 'I am not the parenting sort. I am happy to leave a gift,' he conceded gruffly. 'What's the child to be called?'

'The name you gave it.'

'I did no such thing!'

'Yes you did, in the river apparently.'

Palmer was left no wiser. What had the girl said? He had heard of women losing their minds after childbirth.

'The little girl is to be baptised *Miracle,*' Jane Davenant told him.

'What! You can't call a child that!'

'Well, we shall. Of course, we dropped the first name you gave her – "Bloody Miracle!" did not sound godly...'

Palmer smiled against his will.

'... so miracle she was, and Miracle she shall be.'

It was with a sense of awkwardness that Palmer found himself in church bearing witness, under a false name, that he would help bring up little Miracle in a faith he did not share, standing alongside her godmother Jane Davenant. The baby was happy to express her own opinion loudly as the cold water of salvation touched her skin.

When Palmer pressed some money into the mother's hand, she looked up at him with a gratitude which made him feel even more uneasy. Ellen looked fully recovered and in rude good health. He left her in the practical hands of Mrs Davenant.

'You will come back an' see 'er?' Ellen asked, nodding at the baby in her arms.

Palmer was lost for a convincing lie. John Davenant helped him out.

'God willing,' he said.

Palmer did not believe in long goodbyes. There was little of Miracle to be seen, bound up in her swaddling clothes in the middle of the group seeing him off outside the tavern. He waved a hand then pulled his horse round and set off at a steady jog without looking back.

'Strange man,' John Davenant confided to his wife, without waiting for her response before going about his business.

Palmer left Oxford by its north gate. In the Palace at Woodstock a few miles off, his interview with the Chief Minister was far shorter than the wait he had to see him. He used the time to let Salisbury's official know precisely what he thought of him for nearly breaking his cover.

'If you see me in public,' he said, 'you do not know me.'

When he got into Salisbury, he reported what little extra he had to say, which was that Catesby and his dinner company sounded interesting, and that he hoped to meet him soon through the playwright Ben Jonson.

Salisbury did not appear impressed about Catesby.

'What do you think of Jonson?' he asked.

It was not a standard character reference the politician was after.

'A Catholic by conversion, but not one of the radical sort,' was Palmer's verdict. 'If the majority says white, he will say black, just to be difficult.'

Salisbury seemed pleased with it.

'He says he's counting on you to help fund a play,' Palmer could not resist adding. 'He's looking for a suitably *patriotic* subject.'

Salisbury's smile quickly faded but Palmer's remark seemed to provoke a second thought in him.

'The Latin play we all saw – interesting, all that history about His Majesty's ancestor Banquo, was it not? Someone might look at it – *not* Mr Jonson, I think, because he can be unreliable in his treatment of our friends the Scots and their sensitivities. And a play for the King should be by the King's Men....'

'For whom I understand Jonson has written,' Palmer reminded him.

'But not so well as their chief dramatist.'

Bloody Shakespeare, Palmer thought, why should he get more dripping from the gravy boat?

'As for this Catesby,' Salisbury decided, 'he is known to us of course, but I would expect bigger fish to be at the bottom of this murky pool – Monteagle, Mordaunt, best of all, Northumberland; yes, we would certainly like to pin something on *that* proud Percy. Be aware that we are still playing a game of hide-and-seek with the Jesuit Garnet – we have reason to believe that he may be going west to Wales, as if we did not have enough trouble bubbling away there already.'

'It is as if he is inviting us to take him,' Cecil added as an afterthought.

'And will you?'

'No, not yet. I do not want Garnet for himself, I want the whole cluster of fruit on that particular branch. We must get to the bottom of what is going on. Then I can take Garnet when it suits me.'

Salisbury looked Palmer frankly in the eye.

'... and I *will* take him.'

7

GUIDO FAWKES was not happy with what he saw when he re-inspected the supplies of gunpowder barrelled up in the vault underneath the House of Lords inside Whitehall Palace. With him was another member of the band, Thomas Wintour. Wintour had first recruited the Yorkshireman to the cause in the Low Countries, where he had been fighting for the Spanish. Guido had long become his preferred first name and identity.

Fawkes pointed out evidence of deterioration in the powder.

'Fresh supplies will have to be added.'

The normally taciturn northerner knew that this would not please Mr Catesby – it would mean extra money and added risk in procuring it. He was happy to leave the explanation to Tom Wintour who promised to relay the concern to their leader. Let the gents sort it out among themselves, was Fawkes's view.

He made his way back on his own to Thomas Percy's lodgings nearby. His job was operations, he reminded himself, and if that meant replacement explosives, then so be it. There was plenty of time in hand – the date of the opening of Parliament, they'd heard, had been set back to Tuesday, November 5th on account of the dregs of the plague still prevalent in the capital.

Fawkes was relying on his patience as an experienced campaigner. He was determined to do what had to be done when it had to be done, and otherwise wait out the time. He was not a frequenter of the fleshpots of the town – to be so would increase the possibility of chance discovery by the authorities so he stayed well out of their way. He approved of how Robin Catesby was playing a close hand by keeping their numbers small. That way there was less chance of a slip up, or worse, betrayal.

Fawkes hated London and all it stood for. To his way of thinking, nothing good ever came from the capital, certainly not the error of the new religion and its twisted ways. Yorkshire still held true in great swathes to the old faith. His comrades in the cause – the brothers Wright who'd stood reference for him when Wintour recruited him – and Father Tesimond too – they all had connections with York. They'd gone to the same school. Thomas Percy, whose servant Fawkes was pretending to be, he'd made his career in the north. They both had connections with the same dale in God's own county.

These were men of his tribe, characters who could be trusted when push came to shove, they were the muscle of the undertaking, the men of action. Catesby was made of the same stuff. Wintour? He was less sure of him, a middling man who had yet to prove himself in action. Still, he was the man who'd first thought of the scheme. All the same, it was right that Catesby had taken it forward – Fawkes recognised a leader of men when he saw one. One thing pleased him most of all – there were no southerners involved, what with their nearness to London and the Court. Southerners were soft! All of them!

He went back into the house to sit alone and wait. Tom Wintour would tell him when the fresh explosives were ready to come upriver. Where he got them from and how they were paid for was not Fawkes's concern. He stuck to what he did best.

'There are too few of us to carry the out the plan.'

Catesby stated this as an article of fact. He said it to Wintour and Thomas Percy, way out to the west of the country in Bath where they had arranged to meet. John Grant, he conceded, was building up stores of small arms and ammunition near Stratford in the Midlands.

'.... but we're too few for the uprising which must follow.'

He held back that he was running out of money, despite selling his Stratford home. They needed more men, more material, and above all he needed more money to pay for them, as well as for the extra gunpowder which Wintour had faithfully reported that Fawkes needed.

'Who do you have in mind?' Thomas Percy asked him. The prematurely white-haired relative and retainer of the great Earl of Northumberland rarely spoke.

Catesby kept his ideas to himself, of Ambrose Rookwood for one, a Suffolk man with an unrivalled stable of horses which could be vital in raising the country. He might tell Wintour later – the man was dependable whereas Percy, for all his spareness with words could be rash in what he did say. By all means let Percy bring in his kinsman and employer Northumberland, the powerful Earl, once the deed was done. Northumberland could be just the man to act as Lord Protector for the State and for the young Princess Elizabeth while a Catholic prince was sought for betrothal to her.

'What I want,' Catesby demanded, 'is authority for Tom and me to call in whoever we think best. You know us both well enough to trust my judgement. The fewer people who know the better. Should anything miscarry – God forbid – I for one have no intention of being taken alive!'

'Is there really no chance of aid from Spain?' Percy asked Wintour.

'Best not to count on it,' said Wintour who had travelled to Madrid. 'The Spanish King is not the man his father was, his Government prefers to wait and see, especially in the light of the peace treaty with England last year. We have plans to make

early contact with friendly foreign powers after the event –
France as well as Spain, Rome of course....'

Catesby cut him off impatiently.

'None of this has any bearing on our plan. We are on our
own. Once we act, the rest follows. I am not afraid to die, but if
I go down in the attempt, I am determined that we English
must succeed in bringing England back to the true faith. *We*
are to be the spark. If others have to build the fire upon us in
order to complete the work, so be it.'

He glared fiercely at each of the men around him. He
heard the rumble of assent from them. An autumn of riding
and recruiting lay ahead of him.

It was in a large party that Father Garnet set off on pilgrimage
from Enfield to the other side of the kingdom on the north
coast of Wales. In it were other Jesuit priests and a number of
women, as well as servants and a craftsman expert in the
construction of hiding-places in the houses of supporters on the
way. It was a group conspicuous by its size.

In Buckinghamshire they stopped at the house of the
young Sir Everard and Lady Digby. They were joined there by
Ambrose Rookwood from Suffolk. As he shared Digby's love of
fine clothes, horses and hounds, the two young men, naturally
and quickly, liked each other. To Garnet watching the pair of
them, it was their youthful innocence which struck him most,
so far untroubled by the trials of the world which he knew only
too well. It made him fear for them, and thank God that there
was no sign of Catesby to lead them into temptation.

The party wended west, onto Shrewsbury in the Marches,
on again towards St Winifred at Holywell. This shrine, a
favourite of the old faith for a thousand years, was not openly

proscribed by the authorities – the arm of Government was either too short, or it held itself back. This was Garnet's hope for rest, refreshed by the spiritual purpose of the journey and by the miles he was putting between himself and Catesby's terrible plan.

The wind blew fresh from the sea when they reached within a last walk to their holy aim. For the last twenty miles of pilgrimage the women had walked barefoot. For Garnet, time and worry fell away in this land of a thousand years of ancient certainties unblemished by the heresy of the new faith. With his pilgrims he prayed daily that this heresy should be lifted from their lives.

'Oh Lord, give us back what once was and ever will be once more.'

But if Garnet was keen to stay clear of Catesby, Catesby was equally determined in his own aims and one in particular – he would not allow the Jesuit Superior to withdraw the sanction he had given in the house by the water three months before.

Palmer missed the pilgrims as well. His route back to London from the Midlands was more southerly, this time not by the Oxford road to London but by way of Henley where the old stone bridge spanned the Thames.

Past the town he came across a large wagon broken down by the roadside. A driver stood by it scratching his head, looking at a collapsed rear-offside wheel. The occupants were women, of quality Palmer guessed, from their dress, and by the presence of maidservants getting out of the stricken transport and fussing around the nonplussed driver.

Palmer looked up the road and back. There was no-one else in sight. He spurred his horse forward to the scene of the breakdown, reluctantly compelled to help.

The sight of a single woman at the front of the group made him rein back sharply.

He would have known her anywhere – Emilia Bassano as was, Mrs Lanier, taking command and giving orders. Four years had passed since he had last encountered her. He assumed she did not recognise him at a distance, a man on horseback wrapped up in riding clothes and a travelling hat to ward off the showers of an early autumn day.

She called out for his help – it was an order rather than a request. Palmer wanted more than ever to ride on, but he saw that there was an older woman in the group. There was nothing for it.

'Mrs Lanier,' he called out, keeping it formal, no 'Emilia' like last time, or 'Milly' which she hated, from the lost days of their youth in Kent when she had told him to let her go, to London's half-world and into the bed of one of the most powerful men in the kingdom.

She appeared surprised to hear her name from this stranger.

'Richard Palmer,' he shouted.

She turned away from him then stopped to reconsider, because she had no other choice.

Palmer dismounted. He remembered the conversation with the official in Whitehall, that Emilia Lanier had taken up with female nobility in the country. With the older woman he saw a young girl on the cusp of womanhood, small for her age, a daughter he presumed.

Palmer sized Emilia up. She looked well if a little more matronly, due in part to the respectable clothes she was wearing of a quality better than when he had seen her last. He remembered only too well that her husband had got himself a slice of graft under the new regime. Times had improved for her, for both of them. She was a survivor too.

No friendly greetings were exchanged.

'You can see the problem, Mr Palmer. I am on the way to Cookham with my lady the Countess of Cumberland and her daughter, Lady Anne.'

It was typical of Emilia to lay their identity on with a trowel. Palmer made a polite enough bow in the direction of the two ladies. Wasn't the Earl dead or dying, hadn't his wife been separated from him for some years? Not much liking for the race of men between the women here.

He walked over to the back wheel where the driver was still standing. It was only then that he saw, behind the wagon, the lad, a boy of eleven or twelve. He knew from the bright brown hair exactly who he was – Emilia's bastard boy, the one her husband Lanier had been bribed to give a name to. Sired by a strolling player and not the noble lord Emilia pretended, either of them.

The boy hung back.

Palmer asked him his name.

'Henry,' he answered.

Oh yes, Henry, after the putative father, the old Lord Chamberlain, Lord Hunsdon, patron of an acting company, William Shakespeare's company before they became the King's. Or was it Henry, Lord Southampton? Neither was true. The byblow of a base actor was more like it.

Palmer looked at the wheel in the company of the driver, an old man past his best.

'Do you have any tools?' he asked the man. 'A mallet, a jack?'

A mallet was all there was.

Palmer assessed the problem. He sent the boy off into the woods to look for sticks of wood.

'... doesn't matter if it's fallen, but it mustn't be brittle.'

The boy came back with a good selection. Palmer organised the three males.

'Right lad, you, me and the driver here are going to lift the back corner of the wagon. We'll need one of the women to get the wheel back onto the axle, then I'll knock a makeshift pin in to hold it in place.'

Palmer looked towards Emilia whose sharp look in return quickly disabused him of asking her to help. Instead a sturdy maidservant was sent forward.

The team did as they were told.

'Lift!'

The wagon rose, the wheel went on. Palmer selected a couple of the sticks the boy had brought back and trimmed them with the knife from his boot to form a wedge at one end. He drove each in to the axle hole from opposing ends and wrapped the repair up in a tight strip of a rein which he cut from the harness on one of the horses pulling the wagon.

'Should hold to the next town if you go slowly and the serving women walk,' he said to the driver. 'Well done lad,' he said to the boy who grinned shyly, unused to masculine praise.

So no change there, Palmer reckoned, thinking of stepfather Lanier, the man with the bent nose he had taken pleasure in smashing for him. He rubbed his hands together to shake off the dust as he walked back towards the small group of women.

It was the Countess rather than Emilia who addressed him.

'Mr Palmer, we are very grateful. I understand you knew Mrs Lanier in her youth.'

'You could say that, my lady.'

Palmer's reply clearly annoyed Emilia.

She reached for the Countess's purse on the older woman's instruction. Palmer interrupted her.

'Lady Cumberland, it's not necessary. I am a gentleman.'

... born not made, unlike Lanier he implied, throwing a wicked glance towards Emilia. They would never understand each other.

'Then we shall remember you in our prayers,' the Countess said.

'Amen to that.'

There was a twinkle in Palmer's eye as he said it which he shared with Emilia. She stared him out. Her prayers for him would be lip service only, he realised.

~ 8 ~

THE BOATLOAD of fresh explosives found Guido Fawkes ready and waiting when it pulled upriver towards Whitehall stairs at a quiet time of day. It moored up at the bank below the boundary of a private garden.

Fawkes was quick to open the backdoor to his quarters. Between himself and the two men in the boat, they carried the loads up into the house and stored them in the cellar, away from prying eyes. He counted on the fact that people in the palace were used to seeing stores transported about the place, the bloody fools. No-one bothered them.

'Good work,' Fawkes said to the departing men.

Now all that was left was to work out how and when to transfer the new supplies to the vault below the Parliament chamber.

So far, so good, the old campaigner told himself.

A hundred miles away, riding the roads at night in the midlands, Robin Catesby was carefully avoiding the Jesuit Superior Garnet on his way back from Wales. At the same time he was anxious to pick off members of his pilgrimage. Rookwood and Digby were his targets. They were just the men to raise revolution in the Midlands after the bombing in Whitehall.

As he rode on his way, the moon above in a cloudless sky was suddenly, steadily eclipsed as if by the moving hand of

God, bringing him and his horse to a halt in wonder. The total darkness exhilarated him. What ordinary folk might say signified no good announced itself to him, instead, as a portent, a sign, meaning what? That a great person, a king would likewise be blotted out, what else? And when the moon returned? It would be a new moon for a new world, promising the true faith restored.

Bucked up by the experience, he clattered into Norbrook, the house of John Grant near Stratford, inspired by the light of a renewed moon. His expectations were high.

'What's the progress to report, John?' he asked from the back of his horse.

A man like Fawkes, of few words, Grant took him to a secret store of small arms he had been building up – muskets, pistols, powder and ammunition. Catesby was impressed, it was all good ordnance. At the same time he saw that it was not enough. The two men discussed horses.

'We shall want coursers, able to carry men and weapons over distance,' Catesby said. 'I realise that they are in short supply, and acquiring them might lead to suspicion.'

'Leave that to me,' Grant said. 'I'll take them from the stable at Warwick Castle when the time comes, whether they like it or not!'

Even so, it was not enough. The thought would not leave Catesby's brain.

'Ambrose Rookwood, has he been by?'

Grant raised an eyebrow. Rookwood was a good man, he had horses and money but he was young. The original band were older, most of them implicated in the Essex affair four years ago, they knew that what they were risking was death and more, the ruin of their families if anything went wrong. Grant hoped Catesby knew what he was doing if he was thinking about bringing in youngsters like Rookwood.

'He stayed at Wintour's brother's place over at Huddington on the way up with the pilgrimage,' Grant replied. The house was nearby, both men knew it. 'Digby was with him too. They'll stop here with me like as not on the way back.'

When the pilgrims party came near, Catesby intercepted its advance guard without alerting the main group and Garnet. He rode Rookwood over to one side and told him what he wanted.

There were questions Rookwood wanted answering.

'Is it a just war, Robin?'

'It is a holy war, one of obligation not of choice.'

'What about our friends, I mean those who will be present at the opening of Parliament? I find it hard to cause so much bloodshed among innocent people, it goes against my conscience.'

Catesby overrode him with an easy promise, impossible to deliver.

'We will find a way of making sure that they don't attend. But Ambrose, think, this is God's will. The innocents who die, if it comes to that, they will rest in the Lord. The act we plan is lawful in the eyes of God.'

'Does Father Garnet say so?'

'He does, I have his word on this precise point.'

If it wasn't what the priest had meant, Catesby knew, but the words had been clear. Wasn't it God's Word, however it was received?

Rookwood held out his hand.

'Then of course I'm with you, Robin. Tell me what I can do to help.'

Catesby talked of horses and money, and the need for Rookwood to move west from Suffolk to Stratford, the midland centre of the plan.

'Clopton House might be available for hire. There you'll be close to Grant, while the Wrights are at Lapworth nearby, and the Wintours in Huddington which isn't far away. Together you will have the makings of a powerful force.'

He could feel that his gift of persuasion was still with him.

Next on his list was Everard Digby.

Not yet, he decided.

... which was wise, because when Henry Garnet and his party caught up with Rookwood, the Jesuit was straightaway disturbed by a strange look in the young man's eyes. There was a shining zeal which appeared to want to share a secret with him. He smelled Catesby, he didn't know why or how since he had not seen him. He was about to ask Rookwood outright but something restrained him from speaking. It was a desire not to know.

A deep sense of unease settled once again into the priest's mind.

September was too quiet for Palmer's taste. Either nothing was happening, or far too much, he was not sure which. He paid occasional visits to the Mermaid without finding Jonson.

The Chief Minister would be expecting news, reports, progress, and already the month was shifting season towards October. He decided on one last visit to the Mermaid Tavern. It was a great relief when he found Jonson there in his regular place.

'Ah ! Good to see you, Mr Henry.'

Jonson's greeting also reassured Palmer, as did the sight that the man's tankard had just been filled. For a while the men talked inconsequentialities. Palmer remarked on Jonson's recent absence from his usual haunt.

'Ah yes, well, I had a spot of trouble. The Caledonians who took offence at remarks in my recent play, they got the authorities to invite me for a brief holiday in the Clink – I had to write to all my best- placed friends to get myself out of prison.'

Jonson finished off his beer in one pull. He cocked his head expectantly in Palmer's direction. While Palmer took the hint, Jonson issued an invitation.

'Now I hope you are free Wednesday next, in the evening.'

'I shall make sure I am.'

'Good! Our friend Catesby is giving his dinner, at the Irish Boy – do you know it?'

There wasn't a decent drinking hole in the capital Palmer hadn't been down in his time, for business or pleasure.

'In the Strand,' he confirmed.

'Catesby has lodgings nearby,' said Jonson before adding a time to the date and place.

The company Palmer met there was more than he had expected.

The biggest name on display was Lord Mordaunt, in his title and by the way people treated him. He was a landowner from Bedfordshire. To Palmer he came across as the type who knew how to ply the world and its complications to his own advantage.

'I entertained His Majesty at my country home at great expense in the early days of the reign,' he was happy to tell

Palmer when Jonson introduced him. It was a statement of his position, not the opening of a conversation.

'Talk to Mordaunt' was the advice ambitious Catholics were given according to Jonson, when Palmer spoke to him after the noble lord had moved on, 'but he's one of those who doesn't actually do anything unless it's in his own interest – *I've* never had a penny piece from him.'

As both watched the man glide his way around the assembled company, Palmer made a mental note: was Mordaunt the useful two-way door he was looking for? Salisbury would be interested to know of his connection.

'Will you go to the State Opening of Parliament?' Jonson called across to Mordaunt. It was a loaded question. Some Catholic peers absented themselves on principle.

'November 5th, isn't it?' Mordaunt replied, affecting slight interest. 'I haven't decided. A man has his responsibilities of course. If I do, I will *not* go to the church service beforehand, for reasons I need not explain,' he smiled, looking around at his co-religionists, none of whom attended the rite of the reformed Church.

Palmer looked around the gathering more carefully. There was a brother of the Earl of Northumberland – not a clever man by the way he spoke, what you heard was what you got. Two others were unknown quantities – Thomas Wintour opposite, and Francis Tresham, a name Jonson had mentioned when they first met. From Jonson's attention to him, Palmer remembered Tresham's inheritance and decided that this must be why he was here. Money.

But Catesby now...

Palmer was more and more drawn to him. When they sat down to eat, Catesby dominated at table beyond the responsibilities of a good host and far above his rank. There was no deference in him to his seniors, to Mordaunt, Percy and the like. They gave way to the natural leader in him. Catesby was a man to get his own way, Palmer judged. He had followed men like him into action.

He watched as Catesby turned the full power of his personality onto Mordaunt.

'So you will hang about Parliament in your robes and ermine, waiting for the King and his followers to arrive *reeking* of the heresy of their worship?'

Palmer saw admiration in the eyes of Wintour and Tresham. Percy chortled.

Mordaunt interposed a tolerant hand between himself and his host.

'Render unto Caesar what is Caesar's, Robin.'

Catesby's eyes glittered with contempt. They came to rest on Palmer. This bookseller was no use to him, the eyes quickly appeared to decide, moving on elsewhere.

When the evening broke up, Catesby had a few words for everyone as they left. Mordaunt's reply to his host caught Palmer's careful ear.

'Of course, come and see me, in the country.'

Catesby turned to Tresham. Palmer overheard a snatch of their conversation.

'We must meet soon ... Clerkenwell?'

Palmer watched for a reaction. Whereas Mordaunt had been smooth, Tresham looked nervous. Palmer valued weakness, it was something he could work on.

Nothing passed between Catesby and Percy, which could mean little or much, Palmer decided. From the way Wintour held back, it appeared that he was going on elsewhere with their host.

Catesby turned to the least of his guests, Jonson and Palmer.

'Goodbye Ben, always good to see you.'

'Will you be calling in at the Mermaid?' the writer asked him.

'I may be busy, matters out of town which need my attention.'

When he looked towards Palmer, the investigator closed the window to his mind.

New arrivals at the Town Tavern in Oxford were keeping Mrs Davenant and her new maidservant, Ellen, busy.

'What's actors?' Ellen asked her mistress, of the guests who were expected back soon from their performance for the city fathers.

Jane Davenant explained.

'Like them as comes round at Christmas and Easter?' Ellen asked.

Mrs Davenant laughed.

'Better, I hope, but yes, in a higher form, men whose regular trade it is.'

'What, not 'oliday players then?'

'No, Ellen, servants of the King in London. They've been touring the Midlands because of the recent plague in the capital.'

'I should like to see 'em!'

Jane Davenant could not be angry with the girl.

'You mind your work, young woman, and remember you have a baby to look after. And we don't want another one, not until you have a ring on your finger!'

'Oh, there are men as get 'em cheap by the dozen!' Ellen retorted.

'Now, we expect Mr Shakespeare back earlier than the others,' the mistress told her, 'so be ready to serve him. If it's food he wants, remind cook who she's serving. He'll want a clean plate, and the best meat, lean as possible, not dripping in fat. He's not your hearty appetite sort. As for drink, he'll order what he wants of course, but don't press him as we do with the others, he's a moderate man.'

'Must be important, to go to all this trouble about 'im,' Ellen grumbled.

'He's the playwright for The King's Men,' Mrs Davenant said and then, because it was Ellen she was talking to, 'he writes the stories the actors perform and the King and Queen enjoy.'

'So 'e don't playact like the others, then?'

'Not now. That's why he will be back earlier, once he has seen that everything is going smoothly on the stage. He's not one for hobnobbing longer than he has to afterwards, you know, with the city fathers and their wives. Now, as I said, get on with your work!'

'Fancy gettin' paid to tell stories,' Ellen said over her shoulder as she left.

But she did as she was told when the storyteller arrived looking for food and drink. He was a nice gent, she reckoned from what she saw, clean and tidy, polite in asking for service and not free with his hands even if she saw, in his eyes, that he liked a pretty face. A bit old, what with his balding head, older by a stretch than the Davenants, she guessed, who were old enough as it was.

Still, you never knew. A smile, a curtsey and some friendly service might win her the odd copper in gratitude. She was set on building up a tidy little nest egg on top of her wages. Her best tip so far had been a silver groat, but you had to be careful. Oh, she could spot the saucy types easy enough, and the lechers, they was easy enough to deal with. It was those ones lonely with their travelling, away from wives and family you had to be leary of, them as said how you reminded them of their daughter, which was sometimes what they meant, or thought they did. Men easily mistook kindness for something else, Ellen already understood.

This one though, he was either the decent sort – and some were – or he wasn't a fool.

When her mistress approached him, she went on her way.

'Pretty new serving girl,' she was not there to hear him say.

Jane Davenant told him Ellen's story.

'So the Good Samaritan really does exist,' he said, teasing his hostess. 'And what is the name of this saint?'

Jane Davenant and William Shakespeare had known each other some time – the Davenants came from London originally. She felt free to tell him.

'He goes by the name of Henry, William Henry. Only, we think we heard him called something else, John and I....'

Shakespeare was not particularly interested, not until she spoke the other name.

'... Palmer, we thought it was. But there you are – what's in a name?'

'A pilgrim's name,' Shakespeare said, masking his unease. 'Was there ... a first name?'

'Do you know him?' she asked.

Shakespeare appeared to wave the question away.

'We meet so many people, in London and out on the road. Would he be...?' and he went on to give a fair description of the man.

Jane Davenant agreed.

'He is close to your friend Ben Jonson,' she added.

'To Ben?'

So, big-mouthed Ben had got himself tangled up with a Government agent, he told himself. Ben had a nose for trouble, he was too free with his opinions *and* he had a short fuse.

Richard Palmer, if it was he, was dangerous company to be keeping.

It was worrying news, this and the goings on in Stratford from where he'd just come. There were comings and goings among the gentry, men selling, men hiring more than was usual, and strangers coming in, or so he'd heard among his friends and in the gossip of the taverns. An unwise townsman with known Catholic proclivities appeared to be running their errands. The hated Lord of the Manor was profiting from it, buying up property – and he always bought low, from forced sellers. Who were these sellers? Men like young Robin Catesby. What was forcing their hands? They were mostly men of a type, men who had refused to adapt to the new way.

And there was talk of Jesuit priests hiding in the neighbourhood.

William Shakespeare's policy was to keep his nose out of trouble. If Richard Palmer was sniffing around, then Ben Jonson had to be warned.

9

'ROBERT CATESBY, you say,' said Salisbury, a little disappointed as he listened to Palmer's report which gave the man pride of place among a short list of suspects.

He had hoped for bigger game, preferably the proud, stuttering Earl of Northumberland. The brace to bag for his hunting-mad monarch was sure to be found among the higher-flyers in the political firmament. But the disaffected, impoverished country gentry his agent was serving up to him? He couldn't believe they had the clout for the trouble rumoured on the wind.

'What about Percy, Northumberland's brother? And Mordaunt? They were both there, you said.'

'Catesby is the inspirational figure,' Palmer insisted, who had felt the flame close to.

'And you think you can work on this Francis Tresham character?' Salisbury asked, drawing a positive answer. 'Then we will wait to find out what my official has to say on the connection with Clerkenwell.'

The information which came back was tenuous. There was a relation of Tresham by marriage living there. He was a Catholic peer.

'We usually have him watched,' Salisbury remarked, 'so we will see if Catesby and Tresham show up. Meanwhile, keep after any and all leads, especially those among the nobility,' he instructed Palmer, hoping for meatier prey next time.

Palmer left it a couple of days before going back in search of Jonson at the Mermaid Tavern.

What he saw stopped him in his tracks. Jonson was there, but he was talking to another man. The sight of William Shakespeare made Palmer pause. He hung back in the shadows watching the animated conversation from a safe distance. Whatever was being said, it was disturbing Jonson – his hand was running frantically through his hair.

Palmer thought quickly. Perhaps it was a dispute to do with the playhouses, in which case he might wait out his time or return later – he knew that Jonson, once inside a drinking hole was there for the night. Whatever the choice, instinct nudged at him to leave.

He slipped away.

'A Government agent? You're sure?'

' The description tallies, doesn't it?'

Shakespeare took no pleasure in the statement.

'So what could he be after?' Jonson's blood was running cold at the memory of the supper party at the Irish Boy. 'I'm a Catholic, the authorities know that.'

'Then it's not what you are, but what you know … or *who*.'

'Will, I may be the impulsive sort, all right, hot –headed on occasion, but I am not an innocent. I wouldn't get mixed up in anything to do with….'

'Treason?' Shakespeare mouthed the dangerous word. 'Now think, has this Palmer seen you with anyone else?'

Jonson told Shakespeare about the supper party.

'Catesby?' Shakespeare repeated, as if it was significant.

Jonson's eyes begged an explanation.

'You know he lives near Stratford? Well, I've been home and there's a lot of talk about him.'

'Bad talk?'

'He's very busy with whatever he's up to, and that's what nobody knows. He's sold his house, yet, at the same time, friends of his, *Catholic* friends are moving into the district. He's been riding all over the place, and to be frank Ben, the gossip suggests that it's business to do with the old business.'

The business of religious discontent and trouble. Jonson found it hard to believe.

'No, no, it's not what you think. Look, I shouldn't say this, and I am not supposed to know, but, yes, Robin has been recruiting a company of friends, to serve in Flanders, on the Spanish side. It's not illegal now we're at peace with them.'

'Not yet it isn't, but use your head Ben, is Salisbury likely to approve? Remember, it's not what you do, it's what the Government *says* you do that counts. If they have Catesby written down as a traitor, then God help him ... and anyone close to him.'

Jonson became more agitated.

'Wait till I get hold of this Henry, or Palmer , or whatever his name is,' he growled, clenching his fists.

'No! You steer clear of him. If you run up against him, you smile and you make your excuses, you say nothing about knowing who he is.'

'All right, but I must warn my friends.'

Shakespeare put his hands on his friend's shoulders.

'Stay clear of them too. They won't thank you for the information and if they have it from you, you will be tainted in their eyes. You know nothing, not even what I have told you.'

'But....'

'If Catesby is doing what you say, it's between him and Salisbury. If he's not, if there is something deeper going on, then he and his friends must take their own chance. Do *not* become any further embroiled, Ben, take it from me. Be seen to stay out of it. You already have good relations with Salisbury, keep your fences mended, convince him that you are loyal.'

Shakespeare gripped Jonson by the shoulders for a second time, then went away to his lodgings in Cripplegate. He had done as much as he could. As he walked on his way, he considered his own advice. It might be as well for him to confine his meetings with Jonson to the playhouse for the time being. A man could not, he knew from experience, be too careful who he mixed with.

When Robin Catesby went to meet Francis Tresham the following Monday, money and horses were his purpose. Catesby did not much rate his cousin. Frank had none of the iron will of his late father, perhaps because of it. He was hard to pin down, and when he was, he invariably opposed action. Catesby knew that he would have to override him. He came straight to the point.

'You know why I am here, Frank. You know what we are planning, you must decide, whether you are with us or against us.'

Tresham eyed his cousin warily.

'Robin, I have an issue of conscience about this. How can you be sure that the plan isn't evil in God's eyes?'

'Not evil, holy. I have taken spiritual guidance at the highest level – no, not from the Holy Father, our messenger hasn't yet returned, but I have no doubt what he will say. Father Garnet is clear, if the aim is just, the way to it is too.'

'But Robin, say we succeed in blowing up Parliament, what will happen to us Catholics afterwards? Do we really believe that the survivors will just sit back and let us take from them what they've denied us for fifty years? Why wouldn't they just kill us all?'

'The answer is no different. We must act out of sacred obligation. Many will follow us, too many for the authorities, or those of them that remain ... but this is tedious, Frank. Let me ask you what we want. Firstly, we need money.'

'How much?'

Catesby quoted a huge sum, enough to rent a street of houses for a year. Tresham would have laughed if he had not feared upsetting his cousin.

'Robin, I have nothing like that sort of money.'

'But your inheritance....'

'Oh yes, my inheritance!' Tresham spoke bitterly. 'My father left us mired in debt. I can't blame him, he kept to the faith so the Government crippled us with fines. I am no better than a tenant for life of my estate.'

'You could borrow against your property.'

'And pile up more debt? What about my mother, my sisters, my daughters?'

Catesby was scornful.

'You think too much about the here and now,' he said, raising his voice for the first time. Money was what he needed, not an argument about morality. Yet doubting his cousin's courage would not get him the money he was seeking. He changed his tack.

'Frank, spare us what you can in cash – there may be other prospects open to me. At the very least, help us with horses and a base from which to operate. Your home in the country is close enough to my mother's, and we have others further west. It completes our midland net.'

Tresham thought as quickly as he could. Could he palm off his cousin off?

He made the offer.

'About the larger sum, maybe I can manage it later. Take what I can give you now, and if you'll take my advice as well, use it to disappear overseas, to Flanders for a while. Let's see what the King and Government do or do not do for us in the coming Parliament.'

Catesby clasped his cousin's hand. His mind was running ahead, to Mordaunt and then to the rich and sympathetic Everard Digby. He turned back to Tresham.

'Frank, I need to know that I can count on you.'

'Of course,' Tresham lied to hurry him on his way, 'nothing but a bad cause can make a coward of me!'

Official word came to Palmer in his Clerkenwell lodgings that Tresham was in his neighbourhood. After wrinkling his nose at the slum in which the agent lived, the messenger asked what answer was to be returned – the Chief Minister, he had been instructed to say, gave the investigator power to arrest the suspect and bring him in for questioning.

Palmer decided otherwise.

'No! My respects to my Lord Salisbury, but to do that would be to show our hand. Leave the suspect to me. I will report back within a day.'

On a lonely back street a short time later, Frank Tresham was walking home after his meeting towards his lodgings. He was unprepared for a face he recognised, thrust uncomfortably close to his own. He was unable to put a name to it – it was familiar but in an unfamiliar place. Then he remembered – the bookseller friend of Jonson's from the supper party at the Irish Boy.

'Ah, Mr ... ah ... how good to see you.'

Something in the man's face had changed. It was cold, menacing. What Tresham heard next was entirely unexpected.

'Come with me, no noise and I won't hurt you. What you feel in your gut is the point of my knife.'

Tresham was too astonished to disobey.

They made their way, the prisoner leading on, to a nearby tenement in a deserted street.

'Are you going to...?' Tresham started to say while he was still out in the open air, as if naming his fear would prevent it.

'Make another sound and I will.'

The pair walked up in silence to a chamber on the second floor.

Palmer did not as a rule bring work home.

The light in the room was as it always was, obscure close to darkness. Now it served his purpose in interrogating his prisoner. He kept him standing, disoriented in the middle of the room.

Tresham spoke, fear breaking his voice.

'What do you want from me. Who are you?'

Palmer stayed silent and ominous in the dark.

'What do you want?' Tresham demanded then, when he got no answer, begged.

'I am your secret fear,' Palmer said slowly and deliberately.

He couldn't be that, he couldn't know, he was just some villain out for what he could get, Tresham told himself in an attempt to quiet his own desperation.

'I have money, I can get more,' he burst out. It would be ridiculous to end his life with a knife in his guts in some squalid tenement through a chance misfortune on the open streets.

Palmer did not respond. Tresham could not keep quiet.

'Are you going to kill me?'

The man couldn't know about the conversation with Catesby. Unless he was a devil in disguise?

'What do you mean by this?'

Silence again.

'Tell me what you mean!'

Tresham found it difficult to restrain himself.

'What is my secret fear?'

'You know what it is.'

'Fear of death, fear for my wife, my family?'

All of those were true and the consequence of what he risked in entertaining cousin Robin's mad scheme. All of a sudden Tresham felt faint.

'Can I sit down … please?'

'Stay on your feet!'

The fierceness of the order caused the captive to start shaking.

'We know about you and Catesby.'

'What do you know? Who is we?'

'Your secret fear, Tresham,'

Was this one of Robin's weird tests, just the sort of double check he'd go in for? Tresham was terrified and confused, hoping against hope in the middle of it all.

'We are trial and execution, the dispossession of your heirs, the ruin of your family.'

Tresham felt an awful, cold sensation spreading throughout his body. Tough it out, tough it out. How would Catesby handle this? Imitate him....

'I don't know what you are talking about. I have nothing to hide.'

He hoped the man did not hear the quaver in his voice.

'Nothing to hide? Like a meeting today with a man who is planning treason against the State?'

Tresham felt his knees buckling. Oh Jesu, Jesu, just how much more did the man know? He felt his bladder and bowels threatening to rebel in final humiliation.

'Murder and treason,' the interrogating voice continued.

'I said I would not do it....'

It was not enough. The voice was silent.

'I said that it was evil in God's eyes....'

Nothing.

'For God's sake, the murder of an anointed king!'

Even Salisbury was taken aback by what Palmer had to tell him later that afternoon.

'God in Heaven! His Majesty and Parliament in one massive explosion – it beggars belief!'

'I believe it,' Palmer said. 'I've seen Catesby, I'm certain he is capable of it.'

'I will give orders immediately, we will pick up the suspects and clear the vaults under Parliament house,' the

Chief Minister said, reaching for a pen to write the orders in haste.

Then he stopped.

'No,' he decided aloud, putting the pen down. He looked up at Palmer, eyes gleaming with a different thought.

He got up from his desk.

'We have three weeks before the State Opening. We can place a watch on the gunpowder, pick up whoever is in charge exactly when we want. It is *they* who must wait – *they* have no choice, they *have* to wait for the due date. In the meantime we must organise ourselves, be ready to round up all the insurgents. They will be caught in an act which can bear no interpretation other than treason. We must play out enough rope for them to hang themselves.'

Or find ourselves hoisted on it instead, Palmer reckoned to himself. Why take the risk?

'What is the situation with Tresham?' Salisbury asked him.

'He's about to go back to his country house to close it up and move his family here,' Palmer said. 'I've told him that he does nothing without my say-so. He is to tell me everything he hears or is asked to do.'

'Good, good. I'll deal with him through you.'

Salisbury looked quietly excited. What he was being presented with was an unrepeatable opportunity, to create a honey pot sticky enough to trap the biggest flies buzzing around an insecure kingdom. Catesby and his gang would be arrested but others, like Mordaunt, Monteagle, even Northumberland himself, the bigger beasts, peers of the realm, they too could all be netted in one fell swoop. It was the solution to Catholic militancy once and for all, and it was being handed to him on a plate! Salisbury was as close to elation as his careful nature allowed.

10

SEVENTY MILES to the north, Guido Fawkes was entering an inn in Daventry, a town within the midland net the insurgents were busy constructing. The purpose of Fawkes's excursion out of the capital was an overnight meeting with Thomas Wintour and the Wright brothers.

The Wrights were already there. They stood up, each in turn embracing Fawkes warmly. They went back a long way together, twenty –five years, to school in York. Wintour joined them.

Each reported on progress in turn. Wintour was the last. He had received a letter from Catesby, obliquely phrased but clear to this reader.

'He has recruited Frank Tresham, some money, maybe more to come, and the use of his place at Rushton.'

The three Yorkshiremen exchanged looks. They did not reckon Tresham.

'Let's hope he knows what he's doing,' was all Fawkes said.

Not far south in Bedfordshire, the realisation that his interview with the slippery Lord Mordaunt was proving to be a waste of time put Catesby in a bad temper. He did not bother to disguise it. At the same time, he was careful not to reveal anything. He doubted if he could trust Mordaunt. The man was a taker, not a giver.

'Keep me informed,' Mordaunt called out cheerfully as he waved his unwelcome guest off, south in the direction of Garnet's safehouse in Enfield. He knew trouble when he saw it.

Keeping Mordaunt informed was the last thing Catesby intended to do. The man was worthless. Digby it had to be for the last piece on the chessboard, Digby for more money and arms; and Northumberland for the political leadership after the coup.

He spurred his horse forward without looking back.

In London, Palmer caught Tresham before he could set off for the country. Palmer's orders from Salisbury were precise. He repeated them to his new informer.

'You are to put to your friends the question how Catholic peers are to be warned off from attending the opening of Parliament. And we want all the names, no holding back. Is that understood?'

Tresham understood only too well. The names would be evidence of those who figured as allies in the insurgents' plans.

'You will obviously be concerned for your brothers-in-law.'

Palmer's statement was a warning. Their names, one of them Monteagle's, were not exempt.

'I will look for you in London next week,' he said.

The future of Tresham's family depended on it, he left unsaid.

Frank Tresham caught up with Wintour and Fawkes, back from Daventry, at Garnet's Enfield safehouse where Catesby had already arrived before them.

Catesby took charge of the reporting.

'Everything as it should be with the explosives?'

Fawkes answered with a nod of the head. The supplies had been topped up and transferred to the vault below the target chamber in Parliament.

'What about Princess Elizabeth?' Wintour asked.

'We have John Grant in place within striking distance of her,' Catesby told him.

'Think he can do it?'

'He's a good man, reliable, but I have someone else in mind to lead.'

It had been at the back of his mind for some time – the couth and courtly Everard Digby. He would be the ideal candidate to deal with a frightened princess of the royal blood, the little girl who was to be placed upon the Throne of England. Yes, Digby was the man. They had no need of the flibberty Mordaunts of this world.

Wintour knew better than to ask for a name. His next question took a different line.

'Let us assume that we take the Princess, and that Prince Henry is ... dealt with in the explosion, along with his father. Who is the man who will take over the Government in the interregnum?'

It was a dangerous question.

'Percy is our door to Northumberland,' Catesby said.

'How much does the Earl know?' Wintour asked.

'Nothing I hope, but when our work creates the need for a new order, he is best candidate for Lord Protector, watching over whoever we decide should take the Throne.'

Tresham cleared his throat.

'This brings me to a vital question.'

All eyes in the room turned to him, Fawkes's the coldest of all.

'How are we going to ensure that Northumberland and other friendly peers are not caught up in the explosion? I am bound to be concerned for my brothers-in-law. And what about Mordaunt?'

The memory of his interview with the facile, trimming lord still rankled with Catesby. He put up his hand.

'I would not let him in on the secret for all the money in the world. He would only give us away!'

Catesby looked around the three faces in front of him. Further debate was a waste of time, his look said as plainly as words. He spoke again.

'We have to accept that innocent people *will* die. Even if these Catholic peers were as dear to me as my own son, they will have to take their chance. Their fate is in God's hands.'

Wintour and Tresham dropped their eyes. Tresham tried to hide his bewilderment.

Fawkes's eyes met Catesby's with a look of frank approval.

There were two clear weeks and a few days before the appointed day for the opening of Parliament. Catesby mounted up and headed north to Northamptonshire. His target was Sir Everard Digby.

He found him at a country house, there to celebrate a feast day which served as a notable Jesuit reunion so Garnet was there too. The priest and the crusader circled each other warily among the wider company, staying out of reach. At last the priest summoned up the spirit to confront the younger man.

He adopted the mantle of his office.

'My son, have you made your confession?'

Catesby refused to answer. No, he would not do so until his mission was on the point of finality. Now was not the time. He temporised, hinted that he had.

Garnet did not believe him. And the inexact answer gave him cause for greater fear, a fear which had been mounting in him in previous weeks. People – sensible Catholic women in the main – had confided in him their suspicions and their worries about what was going on – something terrible, and dangerous for more than just the protagonists. He knew it too, but he had consoled them and allayed their fears. All the time he prayed for the return of the messenger from Rome.

Garnet switched from priest to man.

'Robin, I hope that you are not still committed to the path of violence.'

Catesby's eyes flashed.

'I am committed to God's will and to his design for his Church and his People in England!'

The mild Jesuit withstood the shock.

'Then isn't that a matter for God?'

'Yes, yes, through his instruments on earth who have the courage and the faith to *act* as well as to suffer.'

'Christ chose suffering on the cross. He did not raise the People in revolt.'

'I am not the son of God, I am a man, I do what a man can do.'

'Robin, you are God's servant, so you must obey him and his teaching as revealed through Jesus Christ, his Son, our Lord.'

'I believe,' Catesby said with mounting fervour, 'that I am following his will. What did the priests do for Christ, what did they do *to* him? Who were his true disciples? Rough, ordinary men, many of whom paid for their faith with crucifixion.'

Garnet sighed inwardly.

'I do not doubt your sense of *calling*,' he said choosing the word carefully, 'and your willingness to accept the ultimate earthly penalty. But think of all that you are putting at risk! Succeed, and the outcome is still unclear, despite the sacrifice of the innocent, who will be many more than you imagine.'

'You gave me your ruling on that in the summer!'

'I had no idea what you were really asking! And I thought we had an agreement, that we would wait for guidance from the Holy Father through our messenger to Rome.'

Catesby heard the words with grim satisfaction. There was no chance that the man would return in time, not if he had listened to Catesby's advice to take his time.

'If he returns before the State Opening, I shall be the first to want to hear what he has to say.'

'Robin, I do not ask for myself, not even for our holy mission here in England so painstakingly built up over the years, or for the spiritual comfort we bring to the many thousands of the faithful. I do not ask for the young men, and the older ones who have put their trust in you and who will follow you anywhere.'

'Who then?'

'The weaker ones, the women who will lose their men, their homes, their religion if the authorities have anything to do with it. I ask in the name of all the pain they will have to bear themselves, alone.'

Catesby clapped his hands over his ears.

'Women are born to suffering. Our Holy Mother saw her Son crucified. God took my Kate from me, to leave me unburdened to carry out his holy will.'

'Unburdened?' Garnet's voice rose near to anger. 'You have a son! A child! What right have you to inflict disaster on him, and on all those other sons and daughters of those who blindly follow you?'

Catesby thought of his boy living in the care of his grandmother. How old was he, ten? His dying wife's legacy to him. Would he sacrifice him? Yes, if he had to.

He rounded on the Jesuit.

'Blindly follow me? Never blindly! You're the one who's blind. They see, like I do, with the eyes of *revelation*!'

Garnet's hands fretted.

'Robin, I must, as a man of God warn you, of the consequences for your immortal soul.'

He could see that he wasn't getting through.

'Robin, what if you *fail*?'

Catesby thrust his face into the Jesuit's.

'God will not allow it!'

The interview with Garnet reinforced Catesby's urge to surround himself with men of action. After the celebration of the holy day, he rode with Digby towards his nearby estates.

They watched late autumn mists rolling over the fields. Digby was the first to speak, of his good fortune in having money and land, the best wife that any man could wish for, two healthy sons....

'... and the great good fortune that I had the true faith revealed to me when I might have persisted in my heresy.'

Digby was a convert. So too and separately was his wife. His new-found Catholicism had cost him further advancement at Court. James had been impressed by his tall, rangy figure and handsome looks but not by his conversion, so now the young squire spent his time in country pursuits, wondering about his purpose in life.

'You have God's blessing,' Catesby agreed.' Not everyone is so fortunate.'

'No, I know,' Digby admitted. 'I know you have suffered heavily for your beliefs. I hear you've sold your home. If there is anything I can do to help, money….'

Money, the golden word.

'Yes, money, but not for me, for the faith.'

Digby turned in his saddle, fixing trusting eyes on the man he most admired in the world.

'If it's for the faith, you have only to ask.'

Catesby explained to Digby the change he was planning in the fortunes of the Catholic community in England. But it was change which required action.

'I can't say any more,' he said, looking back across the fields.

'How can I help?' Digby asked.

Catesby specified money – Digby promised it – and that Digby should move to a house in the Warwickshire heartland of the plot and recruit an armed band under the guise of a hunting party – Digby agreed. What were his further orders? He should wait for them there. His task to capture Princess Elizabeth where she lived near Coventry, Catesby did not tell him, not yet, only that:

'I shall have a special task for you, Everard.'

Digby asked a precaution, one Catesby had heard before and knew how to answer.

'Has the plan received the blessing of our spiritual advisers?'

'Absolutely and without question!'

Grateful for Digby's 'has' rather than 'does', Catesby answered with a clear conscience. Hadn't he learned the art of equivocation, not saying what you really meant from masters like Garnet? Did not God work in mysterious ways?

~ 11 ~

PALMER had his work cut out to calm the panicky Tresham when he tracked him down in London.

The man was deeply uncomfortable as he passed on the names of the Catholic peers who were in the insurgents' minds to save. Palmer memorised them. They would go down very well with the Chief Minister – they were the sort of names and rank that Salisbury wanted.

He pressed Tresham about the Earl of Northumberland, knowing Salisbury's wishes.

'I can't say,' Tresham blurted out, 'I don't think Northumberland knows, not yet. It's his kinsman Thomas Percy's job to tell him when the time comes.' He explained for what purpose.

Palmer eased his pressure on the terrified man. It was enough to know what the insurgents had in mind for the Earl – the protectorship of a child ruler.

He kept from Tresham Salisbury's second priority. The Chief Minister had been very specific.

'Monteagle now, I want to settle where *he* stands once and for all.'

Monteagle rankled with Salisbury. The man had been prominently involved in the Essex uprising against the old Queen four years before. He had been lucky to escape with a heavy fine, a fine which he had avoided settling.

The ploy to deal with Monteagle was clever, Palmer had to agree.

A mystery letter was to be delivered to him warning him off the opening of Parliament, by using the threat of terror leading to death and destruction. Palmer had the letter with him, copied out by Salisbury's trusted official in a private hand. It was explicit enough and yet suitably veiled in order to give off an aura of mystery.

'If Monteagle alerts me about it, so much the better for him. If he doesn't, then we have him where we want him!' Salisbury had explained.

'What if Monteagle alerts the conspirators as well?'

'We have enough circumstantial evidence as it is – my people have already made a discreet visit to the vault where the explosives are stored. We know who has rented it just as we know who the active members of the plot are are, thanks to your work. If Monteagle sounds the alarm, then we quickly round them all up. Rigorous interrogation' – Palmer remembered the Chief Minister's euphemism long afterwards – 'and a show trial will do the rest.'

Palmer needed to keep Tresham steady for the time being. He was not sorry for the man in front of him, despite knowing that he was likely to go down with all the rest. For all that Palmer had ever witnessed, treason was a fool's game. It was not lost on him that his own background could have put him on the other side; only he would never have been so stupid – or so he told himself.

He lowered his voice to soothe Tresham's growing panic.

'You know nothing, we have never met, what you don't know you can't be suspected of. Play it straight and your comrades will have nothing on you.'

The repeat supper Catesby gave at the Irish Boy did not include Ben Jonson.

Jonson was practising caution, taking his friend Shakespeare's advice, sending back a message to the inviter that he was, unfortunately, busy that night. The place of entertainer at the table was taken by a famous exploration writer. Another guest came from the embassy of a Catholic dominion of Spain. The last place at table was taken by the flexible Lord Mordaunt. There was no loose talk, Catesby made sure of that.

Still, it was interesting company, as a Government spy reported, not quite knowing why, or that Catesby was 'the man'. The connections did not escape the vigilant Salisbury's eye, or its usefulness in embarrassing recent diplomatic 'friends' like Spain, when the time came.

Palmer was on a messenger's mission.

Under cover of darkness, he made his way on foot to Lord Monteagle's mansion in the suburbs at Hoxton. The concocted letter of warning sat safely inside his coat.

It was not a night to be out, moonless and unlit. Palmer shivered – November would be in within the week, four days later the State Opening and the designated appointment with terror. Salisbury was cutting it fine if he wanted to pick up the suspects in advance, Palmer told himself as he made his way on foot, regretting his decision not to hire a horse.

There was no risk of the explosives in Whitehall being allowed to go off, was there? No, not even Government officials could be so stupid as to make a mess of arresting the bombers, could they? Assuming of course that they knew ... Salisbury was the only one who did and he was reliable, wasn't he? The questions reverberated in Palmer's mind as he trudged onwards. Faint fears of a double game began to prick at him. How did he know Salisbury was playing it straight? Was he being set up? If he was, he wouldn't be the first.

He told himself not to be so stupid. Salisbury was bound into the regime, he depended on it for his life and his living, he came from a family of State servants starting with his father who had done the same job for forty years before him. More, he was devoted to the new religion. So he had nothing to gain and everything to lose from the overthrow of the current regime. It was the times which were making him think irrationally, Palmer decided.

He reached Monteagle's place a little before seven. If he had to, he should go in and make himself known was his instruction, but he wasn't to give the letter to a common servant. The text was too sensitive and it had to be sure to get through.

He was saved the trouble. Another man was approaching the door at the same time. Palmer introduced himself, found out that the man was a gentleman of Monteagle's household and handed him the letter addressed to his master. He watched the man go in, then waited outside, hidden in the darkness.

'What's this?'

Monteagle was reluctant to take the letter his man was offering him as he sat eating his supper. He was suspicious. He knew about writs – he was not a rich man and he had creditors. He brushed it away from his hands as if it carried the plague.

'Read it,' he ordered.

His man's voice became more and more incredulous as he did.

'... invent some excuse not to attend Parliament ... there will be a terrible deed ... burn the letter ... into God's holy protection I commend you.'

Monteagle stopped eating, his mouth open in astonishment. His mind worked quickly – a genuine warning? A provocation? He could afford to take no chances. He pushed his plate away.

'Saddle my horse. I'm going to see the Chief Minister.'

His man obeyed.

When Monteagle was gone, his man did something else. He sent a warning message to the Jesuit safehouse in Enfield.

Palmer saw two horses gallop past. His own instructions from Salisbury were to report back to Whitehall once his mission was accomplished.

The Chief Minister appeared pleased with himself when the foot-weary investigator was shown in a couple of hours later. He waved the letter Palmer had so painstakingly delivered.

'Monteagle has been here,' Salisbury said, 'and he has left me this extraordinary and useful document.'

'But....'

Salisbury stopped Palmer with a look of reproach.

'Now understand this. You have never seen this document before. Its provenance is as unknown to you as it is to me. It has come, through Monteagle, from someone close to the conspiracy.'

So this was the second part of the trick, Palmer realised.

'What will you do with it?' he asked.

'The King must be informed, not just yet – he is away hunting and he never likes to be disturbed when he is slaughtering his wild beasts; he returns Wednesday next. We have a lot to find out in the meantime so ... we must let the plot mature.'

'And the letter?'

'I will give it to His Majesty to see what he makes of it. You see,' the diminutive politician said, leaning forward towards Palmer, 'I have learned this much. With royal masters, one must encourage them to come to their own, *wise* conclusions which we ordinary mortals are only too grateful to share, like crumbs from their table.'

'It must be Tresham!'

Thomas Wintour was expressing exactly what Catesby thought as they paced up and down in the garden together in Enfield.

The warning message from Monteagle's man was the blow they had all feared for so long; and it was so close to the appointed date.

'If it is, we must kill him.'

It was a stark statement from the normally measured Wintour. Catesby was, for once, unsure.

'I agree that it looks like it – he's Monteagle's brother-in-law, but we mustn't jump to conclusions, or do something which would draw more attention to us if we are wrong.'

Wintour was not used to hearing caution from Catesby.

'If Monteagle tells Salisbury, then we must delay the plan.'

'No!'

Catesby walked on, followed by a mystified Wintour.

'We have come too far, the opportunity will never recur – so many of God's enemies in one place at one time....' he heard Catesby muttering to himself.

'So many of our friends too,' Wintour reminded him. 'Perhaps it's a sign?'

'No! All the arrangements have been made. Think, Tom, think. Will Salisbury take the warning seriously? Probably. Does he know where the threat will come from? Not yet. He has a dozen different possibilities to consider, more from outside Parliament than in and more likely to be an individual attempt on the King than the scale of what we have planned. By my judgement, we are still ahead of the game. And remember, the main event in London triggers the Catholic rising all over the country.'

'It mightn't be beyond the King's grasp to guess. He's always nervous about his personal safety. Remember, his father was blown to kingdom come in Scotland.'

'Yes, in a private house miles from anywhere in a barely civilised country. Who would suspect the same, in England, in Parliament, in the heart of a royal palace, in the centre of the capital?'

Catesby could see Wintour wavering.

'We see Tresham,' Catesby decided, 'and we get Fawkes to check if the gunpowder has been disturbed in any way. If it hasn't, then they don't know where the threat is coming from.'

Tresham was surprised to be met in a forest clearing on his way to his summons to Enfield, by Catesby and a grim-faced Tom Wintour.

'We have been warned by a friend, a friend in your brother-in-law Monteagle's household that he has received a letter of warning about attending Parliament. This letter may now be with Salisbury.'

Catesby watched Tresham's reaction closely.

Tresham was trying to swallow but his mouth and throat were suddenly too dry. It was clear to him that he was the main suspect – Monteagle was his brother-in-law. So much depended on what he was asked next. He remembered what Palmer had advised him, to deny everything. He struggled to remember his Jesuit-given training, how to manipulate language so that a man said as little as possible which could incriminate him.

'Did you write that letter?' Catesby asked him.

Tresham blinked, with relief. He could answer 'no' in good conscience.

'Did you have anything to do with it?' Wintour asked, broadening the scope.

Define 'anything' Tresham thought, and decided that the answer was 'no'. He'd had no part in the letter. All the same, he realised that he could not rely solely on rebuttal.

'I admit I was worried about Monteagle, but remember, I admitted this to you last time we met. If I'd wanted to warn Monteagle I would hardly have written him a letter, I'd've had a quiet word for God's sake!'

Seeing its effect, Tresham's voice grew bolder.

'Observing the growing climate of persecution against all Catholics, I have come to see that you were right, Robin, that desperate measures were called for. That's why I was persuaded when you saw me in Clerkenwell.'

'And that is where you still stand?' Catesby asked him.

Tresham thought of the shadowy Government agent and what the Government would do to his family.

'Why wouldn't it be?' he said.

His interrogators afforded Tresham the benefit of the doubt with one proviso, which Wintour demanded privately from Catesby afterwards.

'We give him *no* further information and keep him as far away from the operation as possible.'

'I admit he has been a disappointment,' Catesby said.

'Forgive me,' Wintour said, 'but trouble follows him around.'

No news came from London.

Wintour began to think that Catesby was right about the authorities not knowing, despite any revelation of some sort of threat to Salisbury. It was as Catesby said – their plan was safe, it was pre-ordained.

As the end of October approached, the two men rode into London. The time had come, to carry out the final stage in the mission they had planned over months and years. They found Rookwood, Percy and the Wright brothers there. The London team was in place.

Tresham went back to London as well but with the spirit of a dead man walking. He made no contact with the team, nor they with him.

Fawkes checked the explosives. He saw no evidence of tampering.

Catesby smiled at Wintour.

'God is with us,' he said.

~ 12 ~

'**I** want you to keep track of all our suspects,' Salisbury said when Palmer came to him for his next instructions.

It didn't make sense to the agent.

'Which ones in particular?' he asked, knowing that he couldn't follow half a dozen different men at separate addresses. It was dogsbody work anyway, he would only be doubling up on what he was sure Salisbury had already organised. Was the Chief Minister trying to stand him down? The old Palmer would not have cared, would have taken his fee and been grateful for it.

'All right. Tresham's your man,' Salisbury said.

Palmer wrinkled his nose. Tresham was off the scent, his usefulness spent.

'What about Thomas Percy?' he suggested.

Salisbury waved agreement. Percy it was, then.

Further background on Percy came from Salisbury's old official after he consulted his files.

'In his forties, hair almost totally white, a retainer of Henry Percy – nobody calls him Harry – the Earl of Northumberland, that is. Lives in lodgings opposite Parliament. Involved in the previous troubles in the last reign. A royal bodyguard now.'

... so with direct access to the King, a very worrying fact to Palmer's mind. The gamble Salisbury was taking in playing the long game was looking enormous.

Salisbury determined to visit King James in his strongest formation. He went flanked by three Earls holding high offices in the Government, an elf among these heavyweights of State. They knelt and bowed until the King raised them by a gesture of the hand.

'This looks like serious business,' the King joked in his soft Scots accent. It masked his habitual apprehension which the weight of the delegation in front of him was doing nothing to defuse.

Without a word Salisbury handed over the Monteagle letter. The King gave him a second glance and then read it. He looked up, his brow furrowed, then read it again.

'... devise some excuse to shift your attendance at Parliament ... they shall receive a terrible blow ... the danger is past as soon as you have burnt this letter....'

'It must be a joke, Your Majesty,' Salisbury suggested, deliberate in what he said.

'No ... no, no ... I do not think so,' the King replied, perturbed. 'This reference to burning the letter....'

'Majesty?'

'It means more than it says. It might mean powder, explosives, something we know about in Scotland.' He could smell the powder, feel the flames.

'No, no, this is a serious business,' he insisted.

'Your Majesty is far-sighted as ever,' Salisbury said.

Used to Salisbury leading them, the men around him looked at each other in question. The Lord Chamberlain, responsible for security, spoke first.

'Your Majesty, I recommend immediate action, a full sweep and search of all parliamentary buildings.'

The King looked towards his Chief Minister, who already knew what would be found, and where. Salisbury spoke.

'Sire, I think we should be circumspect. We should increase security around your royal person and, yes, we should search the premises, but nearer the time before the State Opening. These would-be regicides, whoever they are, they are criminals much too dangerous to scare off by any precipitate action on our part. We have four days to find out more – my men will work day and night – and rest assured, we will take every precaution before the day in question. The danger cannot come until the fifth.'

The posse of statesmen around him signified their assent. The onus rested on Salisbury after all, the advice was his and his alone.

The King's eyes flickered around them, as if testing the proposal.

'Well, so be it, let us go forward as if nothing has happened. Salisbury, I rely on you to make progress in the meantime. Lord Chamberlain, you are my guarantee failing all else, *all* our guarantee since we shall all be together in the chamber on the day.'

As the Lords bowed and turned to go, the King gave his Chief Minister a signal to remain behind for a last word.

'Catholics?' he asked when they were alone.

'I am afraid so, Your Majesty, it can be the only conclusion, given to whom the letter was addressed.'

The King sighed.

'They are at me all the time to make concessions to them. And this is how they repay me.'

'Some of them,' Salisbury said, who was never one for mass reprisals. Nipping in the bud was his preferred method, and pruning back. 'Only a hardened few.'

'Perhaps you are right,' the King said who liked to be seen as a peacemaker. 'Let us hope to God you are.'

Palmer settled uncomfortably to the routine of watching Percy's house near Parliament. He was not happy, such duties bored him, he would rather be active and on the move.

There was no ideal place to post himself without being seen by the occupants of the house or by other denizens of the Court. The evidence he found of the Palace population being alert to danger in any way was less than Salisbury might like to know. If anything happened there would be hell to pay and a massive tightening up – after the event.

Palmer dealt with the tedium by spelling himself off from time to time. He denied himself the consolation of the tavern. He was on duty, alertness was essential.

He had already established that Thomas Percy did not live in the lodgings which he had taken. He called in from time to time, otherwise spending the nights away. As for the servant in the house, he had learned that he called himself John Johnson – only John Smith would have been more obvious. Palmer watched him closely whenever he came out of doors. The man's routine was the same, a quick glance round, barely perceptible but always made, then a pipe of tobacco in the open air. There was a definite hint of watchfulness about him, careful enough too not to light a pipe near gunpowder, Palmer realised.

There was something vaguely familiar about him as well. Was it because he was ex-military in his dress and ramrod bearing? There were plenty of those around, in private service as bodyguard to some lord or other. Palmer felt that he knew the man, but from where? He racked his brains. The answer would not come. It was not in London, he decided. It was not in Kent either, where he had spent his youth. The only old soldiers there were the broken-down sort in the alehouse cadging money for drink.

The wars in Flanders? Palmer had served his time there. He never talked about them, instead they talked to him, involuntarily in dreams. This man was the type belonging to his nightmares.

Sunday morning came, two days before the State Opening of Parliament.

Palmer at his watching post worried more and more. Was Salisbury cutting it too fine? Church bells dinned out all around him, tuneful, tinny, cracked depending on their age and the skill with which they were being rung. The effect was unharmonious, typical of the times, to the investigator's edgy mind.

A similar sound remembered clicked in Palmer's brain – bells ringing on a Sunday but not in London. Where? Where? Not in England. A town ... in Flanders, a time ... of siege ... and a truce while generals negotiated and soldiers in shirtsleeve order caught up with cleaning and polishing, freed from their trenches, free from fear of enemy action and, for the time being, from death.

Sentry duty just the same for some poor sod.

God knows why he had drawn the short straw, sentry-go that day. It was probably for some misdemeanour. Out front, the enemy was dug in outside the town walls in a trench at the top of an escarpment. He could hear voices from the other side – they weren't Spanish or French. Flemish perhaps? No, if you listened hard you could recognise what they were – English; there were soldiers of fortune or conscience fighting on both sides.

He was bored that Sunday morning.

'Hey, you Englishmen up there!'

'Who wants to know?' a voice came back to him.

Palmer called out his name to hear another one thrown back, English as an apple orchard in Somerset.

'Smoke?' Palmer shouted. Hell, why not.

'You got tobacco?'

'Plenty.'

'Come on up,' the voice shouted back, 'safe conduct, word of honour.'

Palmer had a quick word with the next sentry down the line.

'You're a loonie, Palmer,' the man told him.

He shouted that he was coming over, unarmed.

He flogged up the escarpment under the heat of the sun. At times like this, war was unreal, like a game, today a game suspended. He reached the top where a man came out to greet him looking much like himself, trying to look clean without succeeding and just as English despite fighting for the other side. He was followed by others, anxious for news of home or keen for tobacco.

Palmer shared both, looking around him as he did.

One man was holding back, sitting alone in a corner of the trench, concentrating on cleaning his firearm. He was a man whose best friend was his weapon. He made no sign, said not a word. It had worried Palmer, then, to realise the sort of man he was up against in Flanders fields.

It worried him twice as much now. The man minding Thomas Percy's lodgings opposite was the same sort of man, he was sure.

Thomas Wintour was disturbed for a different reason.

He had picked up a leak that the King and his Councillors had met to discuss a threat to royal security the day before. The news would not be welcome to his comrades.

Tresham must have talked.

When he confronted Tresham with it, the man babbled.

'Tom, you've got to persuade Robin to put all this off.'

Wintour left him to stew in his own fear.

'Bastard Tresham, no son of his father!'

The fierce reaction was Thomas Percy's when he, Wintour and Catesby met later that evening with Fawkes, away from Whitehall. It was Fawkes who had drawn Palmer after him. Lurking in a dark recess outside the room where they were meeting, he was unable to hear what they were saying.

Percy was adamant.

'If we're looking for who betrayed us, then Tresham's the one!'

'Do we go ahead or do we put it off?' Wintour asked.

'Put it off to when?' Percy spat out contemptuously. 'We'll never get an opportunity like this again. I say we go ahead. I am ready to risk everything.'

Catesby had been unusually silent to this point. He would be the decision-maker, the others knew but Percy had an effect on him the others could not match. He spoke.

'Percy is right, we change nothing, we go ahead. They may know something, Tresham may have talked, but if he did, they haven't moved against us, which I find strange.'

'Perhaps they are waiting to catch us in the act?' Wintour suggested.

'Perhaps, but let's examine what we have on our side. The element of surprise? I'm not sure. What I do know is that we have numbers, more than they are expecting, and we are prepared to die in the attempt.'

Catesby examined the faces of each of the men as he spoke, every one returning agreement to him.

'... they may not have reckoned on that. What they don't know either, because Tresham doesn't, is a force Digby is gathering in the Midlands, waiting for the sign from us here in London.'

'Your plan, sir?'

The military voice of question belonged to Fawkes.

'Digby and his force move to Dunchurch – it's only an hour's ride from where Princess Elizabeth lives. Whatever goes off here, he moves in and takes her Tuesday morning. That will be the call to arms for all good Catholics all over the country. It is what will spark the rising we must ignite.'

'The rising will succeed only if the King and Prince Henry die,' Wintour said.

'Yes,' Catesby conceded, 'so we must trust to Fawkes here to do his job with the gunpowder. We couldn't be in better hands.'

Fawkes looked entirely sanguine to the eyes turned on him.

'One last question,' Wintour said. 'Where do things stand with Northumberland? Is he going to the State Opening? He's a Privy Councillor, I don't see how he can avoid it.'

'... unless he's ill, or says he is,' Percy said. 'Leave my kinsman to me. I'll go to him tomorrow to see how things lie – I might be able to find out just what the Councillors do know.'

Palmer was still in the dark when the men came out of the house into the night.

'What time do you plan to go to Syon House tomorrow?' he heard Wintour ask Percy, and the reply, 'late morning.'

Palmer, lurking in a doorway, knew who and where, if not what it meant.

'Interesting, the fox is out in the open,' Salisbury said when Palmer told him the news.

Syon House belonged to the Earl of Northumberland.

'We must assume that this is all part of the plan and that they do not know what we do.'

Who could tell, Palmer said to himself, thinking about the demeanour of the men he had watched. Who was the fox and who the hound?

'There was a lot off to and fro-ing between His Majesty and our senior Councillors yesterday,' Salisbury said. 'The Lord Chamberlain was all for an immediate search of the Parliament building but I managed to dissuade him.'

Salisbury really was playing for high stakes, Palmer thought, the highest.

'My instructions?' he asked.

'Monitor Percy's movements tomorrow but report back to me in the evening,' Salisbury said. 'That is when we will haul our catch in.'

~ 13 ~

PALMER DECIDED to ride to Syon House ahead of Percy's arrival. It called for an early start, riding west into open country outside the capital. It was a brain-numbing experience in the cold November air.

He found the house easily enough, an impressive pile rebuilt in the once fashionable Italian style onto the ruins of an abbey – a stylish monument to the rapacity of some Reformation land-grabber.

He hid himself with his horse in a copse by the roadside from where he could watch the passing traffic. Inactivity began to chill his bones. He pulled his cloak more tightly around him – there was something to be said for city life in winter, he reflected as the waiting time went on; it was warmer by a stretch than the freezing, bone-crumbling country air.

He was beginning to give up hope when he heard the drumming of horsehooves riding at pace. He placed a calming hand on the neck of his mount to keep it still.

The rider who cantered past was easily identifiable – Thomas Percy, white hair visible under his hat. Palmer watched him ride into the estate. There was nothing left other than to wait for him to come out again. The question was, who with or on his own? If on his own, what orders would he be carrying? Percy had to return to London within hours, Palmer reckoned, because the great event must be timed for first thing in the morning if it was to catch the opening of Parliament.

He hunkered down to wait.

'W ... what's the news from London?' Henry Percy, Earl of Northumberland asked the new arrival.

'A lot of hustle and bustle to do with Parliament tomorrow,' Percy replied in a loud voice necessary with the Earl who was nearly deaf in addition to his stutter. 'Will you be there, as a Privy Councillor?'

'Eh? Ah yes, I ... I don't know. I ... I was not f-feeling well this morning, but I ... I expect I shall. I am s-sending a message to h-have my London lodgings ready.'

Thomas Percy said nothing more about it – he was under strict orders from Catesby not to drop any hint of what might be going on; whatever Northumberland's role was to be, it was not to be decided until after the event. But it was good that the Earl was set on going. Late withdrawal from tomorrow's ceremonial by one of England's premier peers might put the authorities into an even greater state of alert.

Did he want his kinsman saved anyway? Thomas Percy was undecided. The man was stubborn – was that an advantage or otherwise in a potential Lord Protector? It was true that they were both family, but he had once been accused of milking his noble cousin's estate for money on the side to help fund the cause. Percy was in two minds about the head of his tribe, who felt much the same about him.

The Earl detained him for a meal and a talk.

Should there be formal union between England and Scotland now that both countries shared a monarch? That was what the Earl wanted to discuss. Thomas Percy was scathing. He was careful not to insult the King with whom the Earl sat in Government. About the Scots who had come south with James he was less polite.

'I can excuse the hard drinking, but the corruption, and the buying and selling of favours by Scotsmen never happier than when they're living off someone else, is a reproach to our nation.'

When the Earl did not respond, Thomas Percy drove his point home.

'We Percys have defended the northern borders against the Scots for hundreds of years. Now we find they've slipped in – through the front door at that – without so much as a by-your-leave!'

'Th-they have H-his M-majesty's leave,' the Earl replied.

Thomas Percy drew back, offended. The Earl was not, except in blood, a man of the north, he lived in the south by choice as well as by Government proscription. It was time to be getting back to London, the angry retainer decided. As for his chief in front of him, he could take his chance with the rest of them when the gunpowder was detonated!

Palmer was feeling like a block of ice by the time he saw Percy coming back. He waited until horse and rider had passed before swinging himself stiffly into the saddle in order to follow them.

It was a bumpy ride – Palmer had his work cut out to keep Percy in view. He assumed that he was heading to Whitehall and the house guarded by 'John Johnson'. He was wrong.

Percy kept to the north of Westminster then swung down Haymarket, past the gothic monument at Charing Cross, centuries old, and onto the Strand where he rode into Northumberland House. It had carried another name, Palmer remembered, four years ago when the Earl of Essex had ridden out from it with a band of armed men in revolt against the old Queen. If they had turned left for Whitehall and Elizabeth instead of right to the City, then his client Salisbury would not be where he was today, or anywhere on earth. And would James have been King?

Man and beast got their breath back, watching where Percy had gone. When it looked as if Percy was here to stay for the night, Palmer made a choice. It was easy for him to pose as a Government messenger and check at the gatehouse whether Northumberland was expected.

He was. Palmer took the news back to the Chief Minister.

Salisbury was not in the best of moods when Palmer got to see him.

But to have it confirmed that Thomas Percy had gone out of his way, on the eve of a coup, to make a special visit to Lord Northumberland cheered the politician up. This was continuing good news. The Earl would find it tricky to deny the obvious conclusion – knowledge of, or conspiracy in the treason which was underway. The plot could not be the work of a group of lightweights working without the backing of a higher power, nobody would believe that.

'We checked the vault, that is, the Lord Chamberlain did,' Salisbury told his agent. 'He took Monteagle with him who seemed very keen to be involved.'

Palmer bet he was given his record.

'Was it useful?'

'Very useful. There was a man there, guarding a great big pile of wood which our men were careful not to disturb – we can guess what is underneath. We checked with the man who rented out the space and he confirmed that the renter is Thomas Percy.'

'Will you make arrests now?' Palmer asked.

'Not immediately.'

Palmer whistled in surprise.

'Why catch the minnows when you want to catch the carp?' Salisbury said. 'I expect more of *them* nearer the striking hour. I am going to put our own team in, led by an experienced man – I have one in mind, he is a magistrate so the arrest will be absolutely by the book. I want no mistakes in the legal procedure.'

Salisbury rehearsed the rest of his plan.

'Our men will go in around midnight to the vault where the gunpowder is stored. I wanted to wait longer but the Lord Chamberlain is getting very nervous about it all. His Majesty said that we should get on with it tonight or he will go ahead with his duties as usual tomorrow morning.'

Palmer told him his suspicions about the type of character 'John Johnson' was – the man guarding the house and the woodpile in the vault were likely one and the same.

'I see,' Salisbury said, grasping the significance, 'so we're dealing with an experienced soldier, not some supernumerary. That does make a difference.'

'Experienced enough to be left to do the job on his own,' Palmer added.

'So what are the others up to?' Salisbury asked.

Fawkes reported the visit by the authorities when Thomas Percy came to him.

'Was it chance, or routine, or something more?' Percy asked him.

'They were calm about it.'

'If they knew, they wouldn't be that.'

'So we go ahead according to plan.'

'I see no reason why not.'

'Good.'

'When Wintour and Wright join us, we say nothing about the people in the vault this afternoon.'

Fawkes obeyed Percy's order.

Wintour and Wright were told that everything was going according to plan. They rehearsed the next steps – Wright was to join Catesby in a ride north to raise the Midlands and join up with Digby and the captured Princess. Ambrose Rookwood was to be in on the ride bringing his handpicked horses. All that remained for Fawkes was to set the fuse for the explosion in the morning. Fuse lit, job done, he was to make for the river and pick up a boat for the continent.

'I will stay in the vault overnight to make sure nothing is disturbed,' Fawkes confirmed.

'What will you do, Percy?' The question came from Wintour.

'North for me, too. I have horses, ready to move in the early hours.'

The men shook hands before they separated. They were so close to their goal that they could almost taste it. Surely only the Devil could baulk them now?

Palmer busied himself preparing for the duties assigned to him by the Chief Minister.

Something was unsettling him.

If he was right about 'John Johnson,' the man was a veteran of the wars, not so different from himself...

... then what were they doing, the two of them, fighting other men's causes? He had taken the King's shilling, he reminded himself, plenty of them of late. He was to be

Salisbury's observer in the armed squad going into the vault to complete the official search. He was not frightened – there would be soldiers aplenty to deal with a single man.

Even so, he could not get 'Johnson' out of his mind.

As he meandered through the Whitehall Palace warren, he thought again and again of the solitary figure cleaning his weapon in the Flanders trench. Whether it was the same man or not, there was a bond between them. Didn't he want to stop what 'John Johnson' was up to? Yes of course.

So what were his own feelings of uncertainty about? Was it because a man should do better than spy and betray? And on his own kind?

After this he would finish with investigating, he began to think as a way to free himself of his doubts, to exonerate his course of action. Then what? He was too old to start again. He supposed he would drink and whore, and waste the rest....

In this awkward mood, he came to the house where 'John Johnson' was getting ready. There was no light in the window. A cautious man would work in the dark, safe from prying eyes.

What if nothing happened, Palmer turned over in his mind, what if the man in the house did not light the fuse but melted away into the night? The search would go ahead – Salisbury would insist on that – the explosives would be discovered, a trail of evidence would point to Percy implicating Northumberland. Tresham would be the first to squeal and bring the others down with him. They would be picked up one by one....

Treason was treason whatever came of it. With the facts as they stood, it would be simple for the Chief Minister and his prosecuting mastiffs to prove guilt.

Did he care about Robin Catesby and the others? If they didn't kill themselves this way, they would find another, martyrs in search of death always did. It was the fate of

'Johnson' which kept pricking at him. Why bother about him? He was the professional, he was paid for the risks he took. For this reason, Palmer understood and respected him. Was it for this reason also that he wanted him to escape?

It would be the simplest thing to walk over to the door of the house and warn him off. 'Johnson' would have a sporting chance, and Palmer could make sure there was no way for him to warn the others. They would be caught in the hunt for the guilty, the one which would round up plenty of the Catholic innocent as well.

Palmer wondered if he could get away with it. He began to walk towards 'Johnson's' door.

'Oi, you!'

A loud voice stopped him in his tracks.

'... whatever your name is!'

The voice was not friendly or sober. Palmer recognised it – Ben Jonson's. He veered away from the house towards the sound of the voice in case the noise brought the other man out.

'I've heard all about you, I know your game!' Jonson hissed.

It was a chance encounter. The writer was on his way to Banqueting House where he was due to meet his partner Inigo Jones about their new Christmas production. He was carrying with him plenty of suggestions from Salisbury, about messages to please the King by praising 'Union'. If the audience could take it, then so could he, Jonson reasoned, thinking of the fee. Somehow it had not made the writing any the easier or quicker. He had no excuses ready for his collaborator....

... but now, here was Henry, or Palmer – or whoever he was. A row with him was much more attractive than a tedious explanation about the work he hadn't done to Inigo Jones.

Palmer came up to him, his finger to his lips demanding silence. Jonson raised his fists. Damn Shakespeare and all his advice to avoid the rogue, he couldn't just let him get away with it!

'I'm not frightened of you!' Jonson said as Palmer came closer.

The two men faced off in the dark. A door opened behind them, yards away. Palmer pulled the writer further back into the shadows. They saw a man emerge, armed, cloaked and carrying a lantern.

'Turn round and piss against the wall,' Palmer ordered, leading by example.

'What the....'

The lantern-bearer's footsteps stopped. All that was left was the sound of one man's stream against the wall, doubled by another's. Palmer began to mumble in drunken Scots gobbledygook. For all intents and purposes they were a pair of Court hangers on, drunk as usual and making a public latrine of a convenient wall.

The footsteps went on their way.

'What is going on?' Ben Jonson hissed.

'Just forget you were here. Tonight is not going to be a good one for people like you.'

~ 14 ~

EVENTS MOVED quickly once Palmer made it to Salisbury's room. 'Johnson' had been disturbed, it was best to act now was his message. The Chief Minister issued orders through his old official, giving him the name of the man he wanted.

'Get him here with his soldiers. Now!'

Salisbury trusted the man he was putting in charge. Knyvvet was a soldier and a magistrate, someone he had known for twenty years, he was a trusted ally. The man arrived quickly and prepared.

Salisbury gave him his orders.

'Take your men to the vault below the House of Lords in Parliament. Palmer here will show you where it is. You are to check it and the surrounding area. We have reason to believe that there is an intruder, one, maybe more, armed and dangerous. Explosives are involved. Arrest whoever you find and bring them back here.'

Salisbury added something more personal.

'Thomas, the stakes could not be higher.'

The commander saluted and went off on his mission closely followed by Palmer.

'How many are there, laddie?' the commander said out of the corner of his mouth as they strode away.

'Just the one, but he's a tough nut, a professional.'

'We'll be ready for him. You done any soldiering, laddie?'

Palmer said he had.

'Then you'll know to leave it to my men, so don't get in their way. Understand?'

The armed company made its way quietly and in good order towards the vault. The commander sent a man forward to try the door.

'Quietly now.'

The man came back.

'Locked sir,' he said in a military whisper loud enough to be heard by his entire company.

'Blast!' the commander exclaimed.

It raised a smile with Palmer. He stepped forward.

'There won't be an official key,' he said, 'the vault's privately owned.'

'Well, why haven't we got it?' the commander complained, smelling a right royal cock up.

He had a point, Palmer thought, since the authorities had checked with the owner that afternoon – Salisbury had told him so. Why hadn't they taken a key?

'Nothing for it -we'll have to break the door down.'

Palmer moved sharply to stop the commander from giving the order. He stepped up close so that he could not be overheard – never countermand a commander in front of his men.

'If we do, he'll run for it, or worse.'

'Worse? What do you mean?'

'Blow the whole place sky high and us with it. What's he got to lose? And if he doesn't, it'll be a warren in there. We'll be giving him a chance to get away.'

'What do you suggest then?'

'Send half your men back through the upper building and down into the vault by the back way, but tell them on no account to startle him into action. We here will try to draw him away from the explosives, make him unlock the door. I have an idea....'

Guido Fawkes looked at his timepiece – it was getting towards midnight. Seven in the morning was the earliest people would start gathering for the State Opening, outside and then in, in the chamber above. The King and his party would arrive afterwards, at some time before nine.

He ran over his plans for one last time.

Wait as long as possible to set the fuse. Be ready for the royal arrival – should be obvious from all the noise and bother – light the touchwood (keep the matches dry overnight), then leave calmly – fifteen minutes before she blows – off to the river, into a boat and on your way.

Strange that such a tiny act, a match to a fuse, should unleash all the powers of hell! He saw it now, as he had seen it times before, a spark turn into a travelling flame, a startling light then the burning, fiery upward surge tearing stone from wood, limb from limb ... and the screams of the dying, astonished or in terror, the stink of saltpetre and the stench of flame-fired flesh....

Only he wouldn't be there, not this time. What could go wrong? Shouldn't be the matches or the fuse, he'd tested them twice. The explosives? Should be fine, the gunpowder top up had not degraded, there was enough and more for the job.

The main risk had to be discovery before the event but he wasn't worried by it – there was a providence in these things. The unexpected visit by Government troops, for example, it hadn't come to anything. Once was unlucky, twice would be something worse. Everything had been carefully planned, down to the last detail. If God helped those who helped themselves,

Fawkes reckoned he had nothing to fear. Nothing would now go wrong.

The believer in him was beginning to take over.

A sound of tapping on the other side of the door drew him back into the present. He put his lantern down out of sight. It was like the tap-tap-tapping of a sapper probing in tunnels. What could it mean here?

Maybe it would go away. He waited. The tapping stopped, then started again. What if some fool was messing around outside? That was the last thing he wanted, it might draw attention – he'd already seen off a pair of drunken Scotchmen as it was. He gave the tapping another chance to stop. On it went, tap, tap, tap....

With a silent curse, Fawkes laid his hand on the lantern and walked towards the door with the minimum of sound. He listened again. Other than the continuous tapping, there was silence. He turned the key in the lock slowly, pulled the door inwards and put his head round the corner.

Strong hands fell on him, and a booming voice.

'Grab 'im lads, don't kill 'im, we want 'im alive!'

Fawkes fell back into the vault, striking out with foot, elbows, knee, head, smashing the bodies on him and around him. Two men reeled back out through the door, to be replaced by others. Other men were running at him from behind – where did they come from?

He felt a stunning blow to the head.

'Sorry sir,' the posse man apologised to the commander, who put a lantern up to the battered face of the bomber.

'It's all right, he'll live.'

For the time being, Palmer thought to himself.

'We keep quiet about the bloody key, laddie,' the commander whispered to Palmer on the way back with the prisoner. 'We took him in the vault, understand?'

They hustled the battered suspect into the King's chamber for the first interrogation. Messengers were already running throughout Whitehall and into the neighbouring Strand where most of the officers of State lodged when in London. Excitement overrode all concerns about secrecy.

'Get your arses out of bed. We've to go and roust out Northumberland. There are intruders in Parliament.'

The agitated caller was a Privy Councillor. He was overheard by one of the Wright brothers.

'We've been discovered!' Kit Wright blurted out, breathless and dishevelled to Wintour when he found him at his inn nearby. Wintour would know what to do, Wright fervently hoped. 'People have gone to Northumberland House, they must be looking for Percy.'

Wintour thought fast.

'Kit, go and check if it's true.'

The man was back inside half an hour to confirm the worst. His eyes pleaded for orders.

'They won't find Percy with the Earl, he's at his lodgings,' Wintour told him.

'On the Grays Inn Road?'

'Yes. Get yourself there and tell him to go, no hanging about – he'll aim for Catesby's mother's place in Northamptonshire. You go with him. Your brother and Catesby should be well on the way already, to Digby as planned. Tell them what's happened, then it's for Robin to decide what to do next. I'll get word to the others in town, Rookwood....'

'Tresham?'

The two men looked at each other. Tresham could shift for himself for whatever he had done to them.

'And you?' Wright asked Wintour.

'I will see it out here,' Wintour said. 'I'll be the eyes and ears. There's still a lot to play for.'

Wintour decided to go where the authorities would least expect him, into the eye of the storm in the Palace of Whitehall. He had to see for himself just how things stood. It didn't look good on the face of it.

He got as far as the Palace gate when he was stopped by an armed guard.

Snatches of talk he heard in the crowd told him the news.

'It's treason....'

'... a plot to blow up the King and the Lords.'

Fawkes must have been taken, Wintour told himself. He turned back to go and pick up his horse. There was no point in staying. He too would run north, north to the Midlands.

Guido Fawkes stood unbowed in front of the King in the Privy Chamber. James was flanked by as many in the Government as could be found to respond to the late night call.

Salisbury had instructed Palmer to stay close by the commander of the arresting party in case they were needed. Palmer watched as the great lords filed in. The deaf Earl of Northumberland looked ill at ease. He must know that the authorities were looking for Thomas Percy. Palmer was glad that he was not in his shoes.

An official voice broke the silence.

'Who are you, what is your name and family, and your faith?'

Fawkes was not frightened.

They were nothing but men in front of him, of the damned infidel sort at that. Some were armed. Laughable! As if the old goats thought they might be called on to defend their King in person! He despised them. He would tell them only what he wanted to. Time mattered, time for the others to get away and to spread armed revolution. God moved in mysterious ways, God would give them time, if he, Fawkes, stood firm.

He spoke up, his voice firm.

'I am called John Johnson, a Catholic from Yorkshire. My father was called Thomas and my mother Edith. I am thirty-six years old.'

He saw the effect the declaration of his religion had among his audience. Quietly he exulted in it.

'A letter was found among your possessions addressed to one Guy Fawkes. Is that your real name?'

'It is an alias I use.'

Which was true in a way. He had been 'Guido' for years in the service of His Catholic Majesty, the King of Spain. 'Guy' he had left behind in England, along with his Englishness, a long time ago.

'You do not deny planning to blow up your King and his Lords and Government, against the laws of Man and God?'

'I don't. And it was the Devil not God who led to my discovery.'

The man who had drawn him out with the sapping ruse? One of the Devil's hands without doubt.

A murmur of outrage was running around the room at his brazen answer.

'W-what's he saying, w-what's he saying?'

The Earl of Northumberland was stuttering on the edge of his own misfortune. Palmer saw Salisbury's triumphant look in Henry Percy's direction.

'You did not think to warn your fellow Catholics, the peers who would have perished if you had succeeded?'

'No, it was enough to pray for them.'

The King signalled his intention to speak. Scots-inflected words pointed his anger.

'How could you plan to *murder* my son, deprive my children of their father and take the lives of so many others, including men of your own *faith*, souls who have never done anything to you to justify such a *hideous* atrocity?'

Fawkes remembered something Catesby used to say.

'A dangerous disease needs a desperate remedy.'

At this borrowed response, the noise of outrage among his interrogators boiled over.

'As for the Scotch bastards among you,' Fawkes shouted over them, enjoying the insult, 'my intention was to blow you right back where you came from!'

'You will be judged, on earth and in heaven!' a voice shouted back.

Fawkes smiled in pity.

'You do not have the power. I do not recognise your authority.'

When they finally took Fawkes away, a mood of sombre reflection settled on the King and his advisers.

'He's the Roman hero of the age,' the King reflected. 'I would not be surprised if he was a Mucius Scaevola, ready to cut off his own hand to spite us.'

'Nobody can resist our interrogation methods for long,' Salisbury said.

'Torture? I don't like it,' James replied. His distaste was genuine.

'But Your Majesty, in such a case of high treason ... and given the sheer murderous intent ... what was it the man himself said? A dangerous disease requires desperate remedies.'

'Well, perhaps. I shall think about it and give you my answer. If I do order it, it will be in writing and I shouldn't want the most extremes forms used, not to start with. I don't approve of racking, except as a last resort.'

Salisbury bowed, knowing he would get his way in the end. James changed the subject, lowering his voice so that one half-deaf man could not hear him.

'Now, what are we going to do about our unfortunate Lord Northumberland?'

Powerful men began to lick their lips. A difficult star was on the wane.

'There's a suggestion that this Johnson is a Catholic priest. They always use aliases.'

The Chief Minister was sounding tempted by the idea back in the privacy of his room.

Palmer realised what Salisbury was saying – a bomber who was an underground priest, foiled while attempting to blow up the King and half the ruling class, now that was potent stuff....

... it just wasn't true.

'I still believe he is a professional soldier,' Palmer said.

'You may well be right. Neither I nor the King have any desire to order a massacre of the Catholics, believe me. We are not going to copy what the French did to their Huguenots.'

'What are my instructions now?' Palmer asked.

Salisbury did not answer the question.

'What do you think Catesby and the others will do?' he asked instead.

'If they're stupid, they will hang about here in some vain hope.'

'And if not?'

'They will keep to the plan.'

'And what is that?'

'I do not know.'

~ 15 ~

AMBROSE ROOKWOOD, the horse master from Suffolk forgotten by Wintour, found himself marooned without orders in London. By the middle of the day, when he saw more and more troop movements around the centre, and still no message came, he knew he had a decision to make.

He saddled his horse, the best in his stable, the rest of which would run behind him as relays. He decided to ride north to join Catesby and the others riding to raise revolution in the Midlands. Rookwood calculated that he could soon catch up with them. The exit route he chose was St Martin's Lane. It offered escape unguarded by wall and gate and Government troops.

In his haste, he nearly forgot his most important treasure. He turned back to retrieve it. An ornate sword, rich in religious imagery which he had commissioned from a reliable Catholic craftsman in the Strand, glinted invitingly at him. He held it up like a crucifix, kissed and then sheathed it before mounting his horse. It gave him hope. All would not be lost if the second part of the plan went well, the raising of thousands of Catholics in the provinces.

He rode carefully at first so as not to attract attention with his pack of horses. They passed safely by the little village of St. Giles. Only then did he give his horses their heads, to gallop in the direction of the village of Highgate. The excitement of the events of the day and the ride ahead created in him a mood of sudden exaltation. If this was his last ride then he would make it his best ever.

Thirty miles danced past in two hours.

In open country he saw a pair of riders ahead of him, Thomas Percy accompanied by Kit Wright, by the look of them. They heard him coming, slowed and turned in their saddles, hands on pistols until they were happy that he was a friend.

'Any news?'

The questioner was Kit Wright. Percy looked lost and uninterested, somewhere between anger and hopelessness.

'Confusion,' Rookwood gasped through the steam pouring out of his horse's hide, white and acrid in the cold air, 'troops everywhere. Where is everybody?'

'We reckon Robin and my brother Jack are up ahead of us. We left Tom in London.'

Rookwood glanced wordlessly in the direction of Percy to Wright.

'Thinks it's all over,' Wright said, not bothering to lower his voice.

'Nonsense!' Rookwood laughed, hoping to lift the older man's spirits. 'We ride on to join the others and to raise the Midlands!'

It took until Daventry was in sight to catch up with Catesby and the other Wright brother, Jack. The men grasped each others' hands in greeting. Even Percy began to look more animated.

Catesby shouted his news.

'We've had fresh horses from Digby – he's at Dunchurch as planned – so we're making for my mother's home at Ashby first. Rob Wintour, Tom's older brother is there. I'll get him to come out and meet me, rather than upset my mother. We haven't time to deal with women's worries just now.'

'What's the situation Robin, what's the plan?' Kit Wright wanted to know.

'We pick up Rob from my mother's then we head over to Dunchurch to join up with Digby and his men. I've no doubt Tom Wintour will catch up with us there. There's John Grant near Stratford – he has weapons and ammunition and plans to get more horses from Warwick Castle. Together we will make a small army. As for London, Fawkes won't have sold himself cheap....'

'There was no sound or sign of any explosion when I left town,' Rookwood said.

Catesby rose to the challenge.

'But who is to say that our sympathisers in London haven't risen, or that the King and Salisbury aren't already dead?'

He spurred his horse forward without looking back, followed by the rest of them.

In Northamptonshire, Robert Wintour was far less sure when he heard Rookwood's news. Worry for his younger brother Tom left behind in London and fear for himself shaped what he said next.

'Don't you think the time has come to give ourselves up and throw ourselves on the King's mercy?'

'Where's the man in you,' Catesby flared back at him. 'The plan remains that we join up with Digby. How many men are with him?'

A hundred, he was told. Less than Catesby had hoped, but still....

'... a good number. We can double and then treble that in Warwick, Stratford, in Shropshire and in Wales. And where the Catholic gentry rise, the ordinary people will follow. Now is not the time to weaken, Rob, your brother hasn't – follow his example!'

The older Wintour could not stand up to him. When he saw Rookwood, Percy and the Wrights ranged solidly behind their leader, he gave in. And it felt safer to him, going with them rather than staying behind to make his excuses to the authorities.

Catesby gave the order.

'We ride to Digby at Dunchurch!'

London was pulled both ways, in fear and riotous celebration.

Government troops paraded in the streets, taking up positions to guard important buildings and gates in and out of the City. The mob lit bonfires of jubilation and demonstrated outside the Spanish embassy. Other embassies reckoned it wise to light sympathising bonfires of their own.

It was all too much for Richard Palmer who made his way to his regular drinking hole, the Bell in Carter Lane. There Ben Jonson gave him a surprise when he appeared out of nowhere. A second surprise saw him bringing beer for both of them into the back room where Palmer was making himself comfortable.

'Saw you in the street outside,' Jonson explained. 'Our little encounter last night, was it what I think it was – the intruder in Parliament,' he said, reducing his voice to a whisper, 'aiming to blow the place up?'

Palmer spoke, only one word, to say yes. Jonson looked genuinely shocked.

'Madness, madness, who could be behind it?'

Palmer picked up his mug of beer.

'Try your friend Mr Catesby for a start.'

'That's ridiculous.'

Jonson believed what he was saying even as Palmer's accusation soured the taste of the beer in his throat. He did not forget how he had introduced this man – Henry, or Palmer according to his friend Will, or whoever – to his country gentleman friend and what that might mean for himself.

Wearily, Palmer made the connections for him, starting with Fawkes and Thomas Percy. He watched Jonson deflate a notch at a time with each link in the chain.

'I'll be damned if anyone thinks that I....'

'That you are what?'

'That I, or any other Catholic like me, who ask for nothing more than to be allowed to practise our faith in peace and quiet, that we would condone, or become involved in....'

He struggled, unusually, for the words.

'Treason?' Palmer suggested.

'How serious was it?'

'Thirty-odd barrels of gunpowder serious.'

' I see.' Jonson appeared stunned. He quickly recovered. 'What can I do to help?'

'It may be too late now.'

'But I have contacts, people in the Catholic community....'

'Who you could inform on?'

'No! There is a priest I know, he's not a fanatic, he could be helpful in getting the word out, nip in the bud what the hotheads may be up to....'

'Tell Salisbury what you know,' Palmer said.

'I will write to him. I *have* heard,' Jonson said without ascribing the intelligence, 'that there have been a lot of comings and goings in the Stratford area. I could find out who was involved.'

Stratford? Odd little place in Palmer's experience, from that first case which took him there in pursuit of the actor

Shakespeare. He felt little enthusiasm. Men would die sooner or later with or without the information Jonson was promising.

'What else should I do?' Jonson asked.

Palmer drank from his mug of beer before speaking.

'You are a praise-writer, Mr Jonson.'

'A sight more than that,' the writer replied, feeling his hackles rise.

'There will be heroes of the hour, Salisbury will see to that.'

'Such as?'

'Oh, the commander who arrested the bomber and – this will make us all laugh – Monteagle; he turned in an important piece of information,' Palmer said, thinking of the letter he had delivered. 'Write them up Mr Jonson, praise them to the skies, let it be seen where you *choose* to stand.'

Names and places quickly found their way to the old official in Salisbury's office and into despatches to the Warwickshire authorities.

Meantime Catesby and his team were making for Everard Digby. At the same time, Thomas Wintour was steadily riding the hundred miles from London towards the Worcestershire home of his brother Robert. The forces that were left were converging on the Midlands.

At the Lion inn in Dunchurch, Catesby found Digby and his band.

'Robin! At last! Welcome!'

They were a hundred strong, as promised, Catholic friends and relatives, together with their servants, all armed.

Digby strode over to greet his friend and mentor warmly. Others in the band were less sure. There was something in the demeanour of the small team led by Catesby which smelled of bad news. The doubters did not like the grim look of white-haired Thomas Percy, or the air of stoic silence which appeared to cloak the group, with the exception of its leader who by contrast was acting with exaggerated high spirits. They watched Catesby take Digby aside. They saw the gesticulations, Catesby doing all the talking, Digby's reaction of surprise, or was it shock?

'I didn't tell you about the Fawkes plan,' Catesby admitted. 'It hasn't gone as we intended, but there are reports that the King and Salisbury are dead, London is in turmoil, people are rallying to our cause. Now is the time to raise the Midlands and the West. Can I count on you?'

Digby stood tall.

'How could you doubt it?'

Others did. Around the inn, men were beginning to disappear, horse's hooves clattering off into the night until Digby's band was half the size. No-one tried to stop them.

The remnant sat down to a meal before preparing to move out. The atmosphere was sombre. Catesby looked preoccupied as he ate. He spoke little if at all.

At eleven at night, within twenty-four hours of the arrest of Guido Fawkes in London, Catesby gave the order.

'Mount up! We ride towards Warwick.'

Warwick was an hour's ride away. He explained his plan to the ringleaders.

'There are horses to be had at the castle which John Grant will undertake, so we go to his house at Norbrook – it's near Stratford – to pick up more weapons and ammunition.'

'What then?' Percy asked, his first words in hours.

Catesby answered him.

'I am sending a message to the priests – Father Garnet and Father Tesimond are at Alcester, on the other side of Stratford.

I am asking them to go back into Wales. I am certain they will be able to raise further support for us there.'

Percy gave a laugh of despair. Rob Wintour spoke up.

'Taking horses from Warwick Castle will create uproar.'

'We need fresh horses,' Catesby insisted.

It was the beginning of a night of exhausting riding.

The message which reached the Jesuit fathers was in the form of a letter, carried by a servant. Garnet's hand shook as he read it.

'What does it say?' Tesimond asked him.

Garnet rubbed his eyes. He controlled his voice with difficulty.

'He has done what we feared. The attempt has failed. He apologises for his rashness but believes that everything is not lost. He wants us to go to Wales to raise fresh support.' The Jesuit Superior shook his head in shocked exasperation. 'We are all finished.'

Tesimond allowed his Superior a moment to compose himself before asking him a question.

'How are you going to respond?'

Father Garnet screwed the letter up. It was a rare surrender to anger.

'I am going to write to him to tell him this – he should give up all this *wickedness* and obey the teachings of the Church. I have no intention of doing what he asks in Wales, or going to join him. My obligation is to minister to our community. I shall go to ground – it won't be the first time. Catesby must accept responsibility for his own actions and take the consequences. God only knows whether our brothers and sisters will escape a dreadful persecution for what he has brought on us all. I blame myself.'

Tesimond had stopped listening.

'I will join them.' The younger priest announced. 'I can help ... in moderating what they do next.'

'Moderating' was not what he really meant, both men knew. Garnet looked at him with mixed feelings – distrust of his motives and admiration for his bravery; or was it that the younger man lacked foresight?

'You must do what your conscience dictates,' the older priest said. 'I will stay here. When Mary Digby hears just what her husband has become involved in, she is going to need all the spiritual comfort I can give her.'

Tesimond paused for thought. If he had a regret, it was the involvement of this young knight and the consequent fate which he and his family faced for his simple act of faith. Was he, the priest in part responsible? He put it out of his mind.

He would go to these warriors of God in his best satin and lace.

The dwindling band of men forded a fast-flowing river, galloping on, cold and wet, through the night to the Grant house near Stratford. Grant was there with the ten extra horses from the castle. They picked up more weapons. They were dead beat when they got to Alcester.

Garnet refused to meet them. Tesimond came out instead.

Catesby kept up his bold face.

'Welcome, Father! You at least are a man after our own heart.'

He embraced his confessor. The priest mounted up on a spare horse between the Wright brothers, men from the same soil in the north.

'I will ride with you for now, but then I must return.'

The band headed towards the Worcester road, aiming for Huddington, home of Robert Wintour. They reached it in the early afternoon. By nightfall they were joined by his brother Thomas after his solitary ride from London.

There was little pleasure in their meeting and time only for a few hours sleep. Before dawn, after a solemn mass celebrated by Father Tesimond, they headed north.

~ 16 ~

PALMER WAS unenthusiastic at the prospect of finding the interrogation room, as the Chief Minister called it, in the Tower of London.

The yeoman warder who led the way was more honest.

'This is our torture chamber, sir, loosens their tongues sooner or later, no pun intended – tongue's the last thing they work on. No, if a few days manacled to the wall don't jiggle 'em up, the rack certainly will.'

Salisbury had been straightforward about what he wanted from his agent when he called him in for fresh instructions.

'His Majesty wants to know who this "John Johnson" is, and whether he is a Papist.'

'He said he was a Catholic,' Palmer said.

'The King means Papist in the legal sense, one who claims the supremacy of the Pope, even in temporal matters, over His Majesty's right to rule. I know that you believe the man is a soldier.'

'I don't believe, I know.'

'Well, that's as may be, but there are plenty who still mark him down as a Jesuit priest. He speaks foreign languages; at one point he tried to make out that he didn't understand English. Now, even if we give you the benefit of the doubt....'

Good of you, Palmer thought.

'... you must still pierce his defences and check his story out. Our interrogators in the Tower know their job, they have full written authority from His Majesty to proceed to the more severe forms of questioning if the gentler ones don't work.

Having seen the obduracy of the man, I don't think they will, not quickly enough.'

'So you want me to play the soft man.'

'Something like that, and you have something up your sleeve, your instinct about a connection with Flanders. Play that right and, if you are right, then we may get the information we need more quickly than otherwise we might. Time *is* of the essence.'

'Nobody holds out against the rack,' the warder said as he opened the door into the theatre of persuasion.

In front of Palmer, 'John Johnson' was stretched out flat on the rack, his hands already attached by stout ropes to the ratchet above his head, his feet to one below. Assistants stood at each end, ready to click up one more turn of joint-breaking agony if their prisoner refused to talk.

From the strain on the prisoner's face, the torture was already well advanced – Palmer smelled the odour of sweat and other bodily evacuations.

The interrogators looked up towards the new arrival. Palmer sought the eyes of the Lieutenant of the Tower, a man of reputation, no doubt doing his duty as he saw it. He knew that Palmer came from the Chief Minister.

The Lieutenant took him to one side.

'Nothing so far. He's been deprived of food and water and kept without sleep. He's had the manacles. We've just started with the rack.'

'Let me try before you go any further,' Palmer said.

The Lieutenant signalled to the men to slacken the tension on the machine.

'We may have met before,' Palmer said to the man stretched out in front of him.

Fawkes said nothing back. He did not look in Palmer's direction but kept his gaze fixed directly above. He recognised his questioner all right, the sapper in the vault the night he was taken but he knew that his duty was to say as little as possible for as long as he could. Silence was his burden. He was trying to visualise Christ and his loneliness in the garden of Gethsemane. It gave him strength.

'We know about Catesby, and Percy and Wintour. We've known for some time. We have other names too.'

Fawkes remained silent and, on his blackened sweating face, unimpressed.

'They're on the run.'

Fawkes twitched a nostril, ran his parched tongue over equally dry lips. Palmer motioned to an assistant to offer the prisoner water which Fawkes accepted, without gratitude. 'On the run' could only mean raising revolution in the Midlands according to the plan, Fawkes believed. It gave him greater strength to resist.

The Lieutenant took Palmer aside again.

'When I spoke to him last night, all he would say was that he was a good Catholic doing what was right for his conscience. He said he had taken an oath with his comrades not to reveal anything. He has also taken their sacrament – wouldn't say who the priest was, only that the priest didn't know what was being planned.'

Palmer returned to the rack.

'One of your comrades has already broken the oath of silence....'

Fawkes appeared to brace himself against the ropes binding his wrists.

'... Tresham,' Palmer said.

A flexing of Fawkes's jaw showed what he had always thought of Mr Francis Tresham.

'Your comrades are clear of the capital. Now whether they are hunted down, or succeed in their plan is frankly beyond any of us here.'

The Lieutenant was not best pleased at what he was hearing. Palmer went on just the same.

'There's nothing more you can do for them or for your cause. The Lieutenant here wants names, or their confirmation, including the names of the priests. Did you know that some people take you for a Jesuit yourself?'

There was a snort from the man on the rack.

'I know you're not,' Palmer said, 'as much as I know that you're not John Johnson either. You see, I know what you are.'

Fawkes's eyes remained fixed towards the ceiling.

'You are a soldier first and foremost. I reckon you have fought in Flanders – a tough school of war, I was there myself. You were hired to do a job. But you should know, as a soldier, when it's time to surrender, when you've done everything in your power and trying to do any more serves nobody's purpose. Not even God's,' Palmer added as an afterthought.

This time Fawkes turned his head to look Palmer straight in the eye.

'Get thee behind me Satan!' he spat out.

He turned his face away from Palmer.

'Get on with it!' he shouted at his tormentors.

Palmer made to leave the room, accompanied by the Lieutenant.

'We'll have to rack him hard,' the officer said.

Palmer paused for a moment despite the urge to leave the terrible place.

'Leave him to think awhile. The more he thinks, the more he may understand that there is no point in suffering any more.'

He only hoped that was true as he left the room and then the Tower, in search of a drink to wash away the feeling of defilement.

In the Mermaid Tavern, Jonson and Shakespeare were talking politics and business, Jonson with particular animation.

'I've been running around protesting my loyalty so much that if I have to say another word about it, I will vomit on the spot. I tell you, Will, it's almost worth being hung, drawn and quartered!'

'Don't make light of it, Ben,' the other man said.

'I don't, I don't. I've written to Salisbury offering to be a conduit to sensible Catholics, and I'm penning some verses in praise of Monteagle as the hero of the hour.'

He put on his actor's voice.

'"The gallant Eagle, soaring up on high / Bears in his beak Treason's discovery" – that's what it's come to, Will, doggerel....'

'Necessary doggerel.'

'I tell you Will, I will be lucky to come out of this unscathed.'

'Then there's no use thinking about it.'

Jonson stopped himself from speaking further. He called for a tapster to refill his empty mug. Shakespeare refused an offer towards his own. It was a time for at least one clear head.

'What else are you working on?' he asked, to change the subject.

Jonson looked evasive. His commission from the Queen for another masque was still not begun. His collaborator, the self-styled 'architect' Inigo Jones – one of those innovators who had designed plenty without ever building anything so far – was going on and on at him to make a start.

'Otherwise how will it be feasible, how will it *conduce* to art?'

Jonson would sacrifice the best of friends if he could make one good joke at their expense, Shakespeare knew only too well. He had suffered from a few himself, including the one onstage in a Jonson play back in the day when Shakespeare had at last got his coat of arms with its motto 'Not without Right.'

'Not without mustard,' Jonson had joked about the yellow background of the emblem.

But Jonson had talent....

'It's a piece to celebrate the marriage of young Essex, the rebel's son,' he heard Jonson begin to explain, about the masque.

... a marriage which signified pardon and restored prosperity for that family, disgraced in Elizabeth's last years. Shakespeare remembered the execution of young Essex's father. He had been forced to watch it alongside the unspeakable Palmer.

'... I'm calling it "Hymenaei" – Greek of course, outside your province, Will – it means marriage celebrations. But the overlying theme is "Union" – union between man and woman, union between England and Scotland. I shall be laying union on with a trowel. It's how the King likes it!'

Shakespeare felt happy leaving this new masque business to Jonson and Jones. There was no scope for it in his own line of business at the Globe – open air performance was not "conducive" to it, as Inigo Jones might have said, and the market for it didn't justify the extravagant cost. He wasn't opposed to fancy scenery and stage machinery. One day he would like to use them in his own work, when the company had the money and an audience ready to pay for it.

'I'm pleased with the idea I have for the anti-masque.' Jonson was still talking. 'I have these characters representing the Four Humours....'

What was it with Jonson and Humours? Shakespeare smiled as if interested.

'... and the Four Affections, the passions which are excited when the Humours are out of balance. They threaten to fight it out and disrupt the marriage until Reason enters and triumphs.'

'As Reason always does,' said Shakespeare.

'I shall be needing professional actors for the god characters....'

The request was implicit.

'The King's Men will be available,' Shakespeare conceded. 'We have been booked for ten plays before Their Majesties at Court. But what about the popular drama, Ben? Can we can tempt you back?'

Jonson was an established name, and names drew crowds. Shakespeare had given this man his first break, on the look-out for talent, as he always was, for one very good reason – the playhouse ate writers up. The days of three plays a year from his own pen were over and the call for twenty and more, every season, half of them new, continued unabated, for the King's Men alone. Yes, it was a downright waste if Jonson was lost to the public stage, was Shakespeare's opinion who knew that his own value to his company lay as much in him finding new work as writing it, and shaping the standards of performance now that he had given up acting onstage. The King's Men had a reputation to live up to. A growing royal family was spawning rival companies.

Jonson picked up on Shakespeare's words.

'I do have an idea. It's set in Venice – London really but we must trip our little dances of deceit with the censor. An old rogue – a great part for Burbage – pretends he's dying and lets three dupes know, separately, that he intends each one to be his heir, depending on what they do for him in the meantime....'

'I imagine it will show all human weakness with coruscating wit.'

'Wonderful word, Will, "*coruscare*", to flash or quiver. But don't mind an old Latin scholar like me. Tell me – rude of me not to ask before – what are you working on yourself?'

'I've reworked the old *King Leir*. It won't end in the same way....'

Jonson laughed.

'It will end badly, you mean.'

Shakespeare smiled.

'I have avoided the all's-well-that-ends-well of the original. I have written something...'

'Truer to life?'

'Oh, deeper than that, I hope.'

'You've lost me there, Will.'

'Perhaps I always have.'

Jonson gazed deep into his beermug. Silence fell between them, until Shakespeare spoke up.

'But since you tell me unity is to the royal taste, a story about the perils of breaking up a kingdom should do well...'

Palmer went in search of Francis Tresham.

'I have nothing more to tell you,' Tresham said when he found him.

'Your bomber had been taken alive,' Palmer told him, 'and your other comrades have run away.'

'They weren't my comrades, you know that.'

'Tell me the bomber's real name,' Palmer demanded.

'What good will it do me? I never believed in the plan, I tried to persuade them against it, God knows. I have a wife, daughters....'

'I will do what I can with the Chief Minister,' Palmer lied to Tresham, aware how little that was.

'His name is Fawkes,' said Tresham, pouring away the last small fact he knew. 'What do I do now?' he asked, hoping for a miracle.

'Stay put, don't run unless you know you can get out of the country for certain; when the Government men come, tell them what you told me. Best case, prison and a heavy fine.'

Palmer did not have to explain the worst. He hurried back to the Tower with the news of a name which would allow the man called Fawkes to unburden himself.

17

THE MISERABLE FLIGHT of the insurgents continued, but without their favoured priest Tesimond. He had decided to make his own escape from the country by other ways, first to London.

'All the Catholic world will hear your story,' he promised Catesby, a story whose final chapter he was not going to be part of with them.

The insurgents' horses stumbled through darkness and driving winter rain. They stopped at last at a property where they helped themselves to money and weapons.

'This is all we want,' Catesby assured bystanders surprised by the arrival of the armed men.

They stood aside, distrusting – not a good sign of the popular support Catesby had so confidently expected.

The insurgents moved on. Gunpowder collected into a wagon dampened in the unceasing rain. It was wetted even more in the fording of another river.

The band numbered no more than a third of the force which had rallied to Digby at Dunchurch. It included unwilling servants hemmed in front and back, hostages to their masters' fates.

Everard Digby was falling back in the riding order, thinking of his wife and sons. Ambrose Rookwood had a wife to think of too, and worry for his horses. Both thought of anything other than to question the judgement of their leader.

The bedraggled party at last reached their destination in Staffordshire. Holbeach House, they decided, was as far as they would go that day, except for a delegation led by Rob Wintour, sent to raise further support from across the county border in Shropshire.

It was repelled with angry words.

'Get off my land!'

Nobody wanted to know them.

The sound of horses following at a distance raised fleeting hopes. These crumbled when it was seen to be a well-armed posse raised after the news of the theft of horses from Warwick Castle and looking for rebels. The men who holed up at Holbeach House now numbered even fewer than those who arrived. For some it had been the final excuse to disappear.

Catesby took charge of the defences. He took comfort from the fact that he had Grant, the Wrights, Percy, Digby and Rookwood at the heart of his force.

'Stable and feed the horses,' he ordered, 'get the weapons inside the house, the gunpowder as well.'

'The powder's wet,' a voice called out.

'Spread it out in front of the fire to dry it. Open the windows, break them if you have to, block the lower parts with whatever you can find – logs, books, anything to protect us from incoming fire.'

The few men left ran to follow his orders. It had been just like this, Catesby remembered, at Essex House nearly five years ago. This time there would be no tame surrender.

He went inside to supervise what was going on.

An almighty roar followed by a scorching wind blew him over.

Picking himself up, dazed, from the floor, he tried to gather what had happened, a dreadful ringing in his ears.

'My eyes, my eyes!'

It was John Grant screaming, blinded in the explosion. Rookwood was staggering around, his hair badly singed. On his own clothes Catesby could smell burning. A blast of gunpowder had shaken the frame of the wood and brick building and everyone inside it. A blaze of fire was racing across the hall along the track of the drying gunpowder, swallowing men in its flare and flame.

'What in God's name....'

The men returning from the fruitless Shropshire expedition swatted down the flames. But it was more than Rob Wintour could take, or Digby either, this final proof that Fate had marked them down for destruction regardless of their cause. In the confusion they slipped away, to escape or to surrender as chance fell to them.

The rest stayed where they were, some injured, some in shock. These last few settled down for the assault by the Government posse.

Thomas Wintour turned to the Wright brothers, coolly cleaning their weapons.

'What do you intend to do?' he asked.

Kit Wright looked up from his work.

'We mean to die here if we have to.'

So the moment had come.

Robert Catesby sat alone, cleaning his sword more than it needed, more than he knew as he addressed a silent prayer.

'Holy Mother of God, if I have I erred in what I have done or in what I have caused my friends to do, if I have offended against God's will or against his holy law, pray for us, Holy Mother Mary, pray for us and intercede on our behalf with him who holds our lives and our souls in his hands. And may Kate, my wife in heaven, pray for me too.

And let me not be disgraced.'

He laid his sword aside and fell asleep.

The attack came at eleven in the morning. It was announced by the smell of burning.

'They've set fire to the outhouses,' Catesby shouted in warning, looking out through a window which commanded the best arc of fire, if they'd had any powder left for their firearms.

The attackers must be looking to panic us out of the building, Catesby told himself – they outnumbered the defenders ten to one but still they held back; were they confused by the lack of defensive fire coming from the house, he wondered?

Thomas Percy laughed, brought back to life by the danger.

'They don't know we have no powder.'

Stooped behind a protecting wall, the posse commander was confused. Were the defenders holding fire until his men went in? He complained as much to his second-in-command.

Neither fancied what was in front of them just as much as they knew that they could not afford to leave the matter to the flames burning closer to the house – Whitehall would expect some of the rebels to be taken alive. Government casualties were a secondary consideration, to Whitehall.

Inside the house, Catesby saw that his small band of defenders was beginning to unsettle. Whatever was to come, they wanted it now.

'They will rush us any minute,' he shouted. 'We mustn't be caught like rats in a hole. Our best chance is to take them on, hand to hand out front in the courtyard. We can fight our way through and make our getaway!'

He was interrupted by a shout going up outside, the sound of their attackers giving themselves the courage to attack.

'Now!' Catesby ordered.

Thomas Wintour was first out of the door and into open space. The crack of a single musket saw him stagger, his sword arm hanging uselessly from a searing wound in the shoulder.

Following him out, the Wrights went down one after the other, shot like rabbits – they lay where they fell, barely moving. Last man out, Rookwood, took a gunshot wound which disabled but did not kill him.

Behind the door, Catesby looked at Thomas Percy.

'Time to go, Thomas.'

The older man looked back at him.

'Together then.'

They edged out of the door, bodies wedged closely together.

They saw Wintour staggering around outside like some crippled farmyard animal after a botched attempt at killing.

'Over here, Tom.'

'My sword arm is useless!'

'Stand by us and we will die together.'

They formed a trinity in the doorway. A musketeer saw his chance and fired, a plume of smoke obscuring his face as the weapon recoiled into his shoulder.

Percy grunted and fell, hit by a ball which had blasted right through Catesby and dumped him soundlessly on the ground. Percy lay slumped, unable to move, breathing heavily. Wintour, untouched, useless in his own defence, saw Catesby crawl back through the door. He heard the encouraged roar of the attackers, saw them rush in across the yard. One man came at him with a pike, fear, anger and brute determination mixed up in his face. Wintour tried to swat it away with his weaker arm. He felt the breathtaking slice of the blade carve into his gut and the vomit in his throat before half-fainting. Troops crashing past him into the house slithered by him, their boots slipping on the blood pooled in the doorway.

He rolled over in emasculated agony to look behind him through the door. Inside Catesby was prostrate and unmoving, clutching an image of the Virgin Mary.

Catesby was dead when they found him, or so the attackers reported.

Grant, Rookwood and Wintour were taken alive, blinded, wounded by bullet or gaffed. The Wrights and Thomas Percy died when the posse ransacked their bodies for weapons, money, and their silken underclothes.

Looking down on their bodies, white and gored on the ground, the commander was unmoved.

'Whitehall should be pleased,' he said, thinking of the report he would send in, of the men captured as well as those killed.

It got even better for the Government men – Digby was picked up soon after in the surrounding country. Robert Wintour went on the run. It would be two months before he was betrayed and captured, the older brother who had never really believed.

There were no casualties on the Government side.

It was a sordid end to God's work, Thomas Wintour had time to reflect between jolts of pain in the cart in which he was being carried, on the road to the horrors which would come next.

Palmer heard the speech of King James in Parliament hidden at the back of the retinue of his client the Earl of Salisbury.

The King was angry.

'This was destruction prepared not only for me but for all of you here present,' he began ominously, drawing everyone together as his indignation spread through the listening crowd; 'sparing neither rank, age or sex – not so much a crying sin of blood,' James pronounced, cranking up the volume, 'no, a *roaring,* no, a *thun-der-ing sin,* of *fire* and *brimstone,* from which God has so miraculously delivered us all.'

Was it from a child's memories of the furious John Knox that the King had taken his style today?

'And the fearful cruelty! It would have taken the whole nobility, all the clergy, most of the knights and gentry, all the judges of the land, the lawyers and the clerks.'

Looking on, Palmer wasn't so sure this was such a bad thing.

'And the wretch in the Tower confesses that it was purposely planned by them to be done in this House where the cruel laws – as they call them – were made against their religion.'

Palmer turned his mind to the man on the rack, and to his own father whose lands had been expropriated for opposing these laws which the King no doubt considered just, as did most of the people assembled. As for the law-abiding Catholics present, they were no doubt like him, keeping their heads down and their mouths firmly shut.

As if to answer the question, the King lowered his voice without sacrificing its sonority.

'But if the zeal in your hearts might lead you rashly to blame those who may be innocent of this attempt, I should be sorry if the innocent, either at home or abroad, should be blamed or harmed in consequence. Though it cannot be denied that it was the blind superstition in their error of religion that led them to this desperate plan' – a knowing look from the King kept the prejudices of most of the crowd with him – 'it does not follow that all who profess the religion of Rome are guilty of the same.'

Was there a breath of relief from the minority present? Palmer detected a pause as the majority struggled to know how to react until a groundswell of support slowly built up with murmurings of assent led by Salisbury and his faction.

So there was to be no mass persecution of the Catholics or blame on them or their religion. There was no blame laid either at the doors of foreign Catholic powers. The atrocity was placed firmly on the heads of a few fanatics castigated by the King for their pitilessness in targeting young and old alike, and their use of the terrifying instrument of fire.

Was 'no recrimination' the text for the day? Palmer did not think so – the authorities would not leave it there. Lives might be spared but property and the means of living would not. Vultures would swoop down and settle on what was left of the worldly livings of the offenders. That had been the experience of Palmer the father, visited on his son.

'Very satisfying all round,' was Salisbury's verdict when he finally had time to talk to his agent later in the day. 'We are getting chapter and verse from our captive at last' – Palmer had no need to imagine how – 'and the surviving insurgents will be brought down to London next week, along with the heads of those already killed. Public display should make the lunatic few think again.'

The Chief Minister did not have an improving view of human nature.

'There is more to be done of course. A few are still on the run, the man – what is he called? Tresham? is being picked up.'

'Is he worth it?' Palmer asked. 'He was helpful to us.'

'Under duress, under duress.'

Palmer did not answer. Salisbury looked him closely in the eye.

'Do not weaken, my friend. You're no use to me if you do. Tresham *will* be picked up and then he will have to take his chance. Our agents are on their way to the Jesuit safehouse in Enfield, and to the homes of the other insurgents in the Midlands.'

If confirmed to Palmer what he had already thought, this search for the guilty and the punishment of the innocent among the women and children. Old family experience of dispossession by the State tugged at his memory.

'You think I am being ruthless?' Salisbury asked him. 'Let me tell you, there are those who would raze these people's houses to the ground as an example.'

... as opposed to the softer sort who contented themselves with expropriating the property for themselves instead? Palmer said nothing more.

'Do not think that we shall not reach up into our own kind to root out treachery,' Salisbury said. 'Yes, we will have Tresham but we will also have Mordaunt and, this time, without a shadow of a doubt, Northumberland!'

The last name appeared to give Salisbury especial pleasure.

'The King has prorogued Parliament until the end of January, so, while His Majesty enjoys his hunting and gives thanks to Almighty God for safe deliverance, we have work to do. There is the matter of a publication we have in mind, to be filled with confessions of the ringleaders and formal interrogations of suspects, all very useful for feeding the maw of public opinion.'

At least writing and printing were not his trade, Palmer consoled himself.

'The fighting wing of the insurgency has been crushed, but there remains the deeper ill, the true inspiration behind the movement. I mean of course....'

'The priests?'

'The Jesuits are still at large. The head of the recognised Catholic priesthood in England, the one we have always been able to do business with – *unlike* the Jesuits – he has issued a statement disassociating himself from the radicals and rejecting violence. We may even persuade them into a new oath of allegiance to the King, to resolve once and for all the so-called supremacy of the Pope in Catholic eyes. But while the Jesuits are free and active, I doubt if such a move can be as effective as we would wish. So there is another job for you.'

Palmer waited to hear what he could not refuse. His family had a recusant past, he himself had mixed with the insurgents. It would not take much to alter the complexion of his involvement if he upset the authorities. He would not be the first agent or the last to find himself compromised. Besides, there was the money. He listened to Salisbury's instruction.

'If we assume that our agents find no-one in Enfield, then they will move onto the Digby place and others nearby to dig these Jesuits out. I want my own man on the spot – you. I want these captured priests alive, so we must control any local over-enthusiasm or calls for local jurisdiction. Do this and I will have a more beneficial proposal for you when all this is over.'

Palmer sniffed perks in the air. Well, one last push couldn't hurt, he told himself.

18

WITH MONEY burning a hole in his pockets, Palmer spent it freely in the Bell Inn. Bored with that, he took himself off to look at new lodgings. He found an old monastery now in private hands with gentlemen's chambers for rent. He selected one and made payment for the quarter in advance.

For the first time in his career he went to bank money with a goldsmith on Cheapside. But his newfound status made him no more comfortable than the new bed in his new lodgings.

At the end of the month, he treated himself to a copy of the Government's account of the plot from a stall in St Paul's churchyard. It was quickly becoming a bestseller.

Not far away at the Mermaid Tavern on Bread Street, another reader was discussing the same book over a tankard of best beer.

'There's matter in this somewhere, but I'm damned if I'm going to risk my neck digging it out. I'm in enough trouble as it is,' Ben Jonson said, 'and I've got too much on with the masque.'

William Shakespeare passed the publication back.

'"The rarest sort of monsters" – colourful language to use for the arrested men.'

'It's a powerful image, Will, you ought to be able to do something with it.'

And he might well, Shakespeare privately agreed, even if one of the 'monsters,' John Grant was a man he knew in Stratford and had trusted in business. It was a fact he decided not to share with his friend, or with anyone. He moved the subject carefully away from recent events.

'I have been scouring the old chronicles for a suitable story with a Scottish flavour. The King's Men are required to produce something which will proclaim the King's pedigree, but I need a story, a frame to work within....'

Jonson had an idea.

'There was a piece put on in Oxford during the royal visit in the summer – I didn't see it but I heard about it.' From Palmer, he recalled. Well, better not mention him. 'It harked back to some ancestor of the king's, odd name, begins with a "B". Three Sybils prophesy that this "B" character will father the Stuart line....'

'Roman prophetesses are too obscure for our audience at the Globe.'

'Well, witches then – I had witches in my masque last year, a scabby bunch. The King loved them – he is fascinated by witches, he even wrote a book on the subject; that royal arse-licker Inigo Jones told me as much.'

'So, three witches,' Shakespeare reflected, 'foretelling great things, or maybe ... something which is not what it seems.'

Jonson laughed.

'I'll give you this, Will, you're no plot-maker but you usually bend the one you find into another form! You are protean, my friend, a shapeshifter!'

'Ancestor with a name beginning with "B", you say?' said Shakespeare.

It was a better Christmas than Palmer had enjoyed for years. He did not forget Ellen in Oxford and her brat. He had a small package made up, a simple toy for the child with some candied fruit and a silver sixpence for the girl-mother which he sent down to Oxford. The landlord at the Bell Inn who consigned it

to the carriers was impressed at the upturn in the investigator's
fortunes.

'Much more of this and it won't be "Dick" no longer,' the
landlord said, 'it'll be Mr Palmer, livin' like a gen'l'man, that's
for sure, like he says he once was.'

An evening of truce at the Mermaid with Ben Jonson
produced a surprise invitation in return.

'Guest entrance to my new masque,' the writer said to
Palmer, 'on the eleventh night of Christmas, in the Banqueting
House in the gracious presence of....'

... of the King and Queen was what he meant.

Must have been drunk to agree, Palmer thought when it
came to the following morning. He hadn't been to the
Banqueting House before. When he got there on the due night,
he found it to be a draughty old tent, painted canvas held up by
wooden poles warmed by nothing more than the bodies in the
audience. It had been temporary in the old Queen's time when
it was put up a generation ago. A lick of paint, in the form of a
fresh roof scene showing vigorous clouds did little to improve
it. Luckily it was a full house. Palmer was, he saw, in possession
of an exclusive invitation. Looking around at a crowd far more
fashionable than he was used to, he smelled the reek of heavy
perfume over the usual rancid sweat.

Heads were swivelling and not towards him. Music struck
up boldly to greet the royal party, the Queen animated, the
King more reluctant, following on behind his consort as they
took their places on a special platform. Palmer noticed how
awkwardly the King moved, off-balance. That he looked better
on four legs on a horse rather than on his own two, was a joke
currently doing the rounds.

All eyes turned to the stage in the middle of the arena. At
its centre was a Roman altar lettered in gold with the brazen
claim of 'Union'. Behind it, like an oversized moon, a large

globe, seemingly poised in mid air, was in fact suspended by a hawser from the roof. There it hung, flanked by golden statues of Greek mythical figures. The startling blue of the globe was touched up by silver waves. Behind the stage, sky and clouds painted on a rear curtain were amplified by mirrors and pockets of light artfully deployed to make their picture larger.

Palmer had seen nothing like this gleaming artificial creation before. In the public theatre, the only visual splendour was in the actors' hand-me-down costumes from their noble patrons.

'I see Mr Jones is in Italian mood,' a voice next to him piped up. Its owner looked a strange character, old and at the same time ageless, scruffily dressed. He introduced himself to Palmer as 'a criticaster, or critic as we say amongst ourselves'.

It was a function Palmer found hard to understand when he made the mistake of asking. The man's job was 'to inform – and educate – the public taste', or so he said.

'Yes, definitely Italian,' the critic repeated. 'Mr Jones's style has been brought back from his travels there, inspired, I should say, by Roman and Greek models, as we can see.'

The audience hushed, but not completely. A stately figure – 'Hymen, God of Marriage,' the critic whispered in Palmer's ear – was slowly advancing on the stage. One of the King's Men, Palmer recognised without being able to put a name to him. His robes were dyed in a saffron shade which even Palmer knew to be all the rage, imported from France. Behind the God came a young couple robed in white, boy actors representing the newly-weds in whose honour the masque was being given. A chorus behind them presented the theme for the evening.

'*Union*, mistress of these rites
Will be observed with eyes
As simple as her nights.'

Hymen – another King's Man from his confident declamation and stage bearing – was soon ladling flattery on the royal couple, for 'gracing Union'.

'From what I hear, the regularity of union between Their Majesties is a matter of some speculation. Then again, there are four royal children and another on the way.'

Palmer was astonished – had he heard right what his neighbour said? He looked around to see if anyone else had noticed. It was dangerous talk which he did not want to be associated with. His glance caught someone else's in the crowd who pretended not to recognise him – the other playwright, William Shakespeare wasn't it? There to keep an eye on his actors and to check out the appeal of the masque, no doubt. Actors were never averse to borrowing....

At the back of the stage the suspended globe began to swivel. And the man doing the pushing was none other than Mr Ben Jonson himself, masquerading as the genius of the place!

'Mr Jones's famous machina versatilis,' the critic confided, 'which means....'

'Yes, I know what it means,' Palmer snapped back.

The globe swung round to gasps of appreciation from the audience and effort from Ben Jonson. Its reverse was hollowed-out and filled by....

'....six, seven, *eight* men,' Palmer counted.

'... representing the Humours and Affections,' the critic explained.

The men swarmed out of the shell. Half of them stamped and thrust in choreographed movement set to discordant music, threatening to break up the wedding. They were young courtiers, Palmer could see, each one turning the best stockinged leg he could to please the King.

With a grand gesture, a noble figure appeared above to quell their disturbance.

'Pacifying Reason,' the critic whispered.

Another King's Man, Palmer reckoned, watching the figure dressed in cloth of blue shimmering with stars, arm outstretched, hand pointing down.

'A man of course. In Italy, they encourage women to act as well as dance on the stage.' The sneer in the critic's voice betrayed exactly what he thought of that!

Reason spoke out, intoning the joys of married love. The critic snorted.

The cloud-flecked backcloth parted. The Goddess Juno, in sumptuous, classical costume, joined in the staged composition.

'Patroness of Marriage,' said the critic.

'I *know* that,' Palmer said.

Beneath the Goddess, drifting down from the heavens an octet of female dancers formed a circle to bless and protect the young married couple. They were ladies of the Court, in tight-fitting bodices above flowing dancing skirts.

The critic perched forward in his seat at the promise of glimpses of ankles.

'Mr Jones *has* excelled himself,' he pronounced.

What about Mr Jonson, Palmer wondered? What about the words?

Onstage, men and women began to dance an interlude. The music was attractive, Palmer conceded.

'Women may of course dance,' the critic said, 'indeed, Her Majesty often appears in the masque herself. But women may not commit the vulgarity of speaking.'

The men appeared to be as lissom as the women.

'His Majesty appreciates beauty in both sexes.'

The young dancers were performing well, if it wasn't for a self-regarding look among the men directed to family and friends in the audience who in turn were pointing and waving back. It was what you got with those who did not earn their living from the stage, Palmer surprised himself in thinking. God forbid he should turn into – what was it? – a critic.

Soon his backside was longing for respite.

He was hopeful when the musicians struck up a piece anticipating the marital pleasures of the night but Reason delayed them – unreasonably, Palmer wanted to say, buttocks aching – with the command that the young couples....

'... with grateful honours thank his Grace
that hath so gloriously glorified the place.'

Palmer looked over his shoulder at King James on his throne. Was he sleeping? Not the Queen, she was nodding benignly at this latest bucketful of flattery.

Palmer's neighbour drew him back with another semi-public pronouncement.

'His Majesty gets quite short-tempered if the authors don't introduce the dancing early. All that now remains is the song to the bride, or epithalamion, as we should correctly call it.'

Palmer, who knew perfectly well what an epithalamion was, bristled in his place. The critic was undeterred.

'It is the writer's pride and joy, I'm reliably informed, all fifteen verses of it.'

Oh God! Fifteen verses!

But the song ended after only one, which came as a great relief to Palmer and his aching flesh. Who had decided on the cut, he wondered? Jonson surely, but would he have cut his own verse?

A dazzling light exploded throughout the auditorium, prompting the audience into applause. Chatter swelled as bodies stood and stretched after three hours of cold, uninterrupted spectacle.

Well, fancy that, Palmer thought. Perhaps the King thought the same given the visible speed with which he was leaving the tent. He wondered if he shouldn't do the same, to avoid visiting Jonson behind the scenes as the writer had suggested he might. Whatever did one say on these occasions? Palmer was no good at the lie direct.

What he really wanted was a drink. He turned towards his neighbour, but he was already gone. Delicious young men and women performers to congratulate perhaps? Palmer aimed for the exit. Just short of the door, an older woman deliberately caught his eye, of a very different demeanour to what had just been seen onstage.

'We prayed for you, Mr Palmer.'

For a moment Palmer could not place her until he remembered where, far from London and the splendour of the court. It was Lady Cumberland – from the breakdown on the road outside Henley. He looked around for the waiting woman he was sure would be with her. Emilia Lanier would not miss the glamour of a Court entertainment. It was the world she was born for.

He was not mistaken. Lady Cumberland gracefully indicated a companion half-hidden behind her. She left Emilia Lanier and him together.

'Lady Cumberland knows all about our *connection*,' Emilia said after looking carefully around her to check that those near to them were busy with conversations of their own.

'... she has been my salvation.'

The religiosity irked Palmer. It was in marked contrast to the fashionable style of her dress.

'... she has borne, with the patience of Christ the crosses in her troubled path through life.'

Palmer knew the London gossip about the Countess's separation from her husband. He was a better sea-commander than he was a gambler, said to be in a bad way and nearing the end.

'... I live now for God.'

Had everything in her life had been confessed to the wise and forgiving lady she was now companion to?

'... and for my boy, of course. I have had...'

... a vision, she wanted to say but she kept the word back. It was a vision of the passion of Christ and the women who had wept for him and cared for his broken body. It paired the virtues of these women with those of the Redeemer of Sins. Were not sins, including her own, inflicted in the main by men upon women? Lady Cumberland and her peers had encouraged her when she said she might write these visions down in verse.

But the man opposite her was unredeemable, she decided, and therefore closed to visions.

'I have had ... good *fortune*,' she said instead.

It only needed Palmer to say something pleasant to her. But he could not.

She switched the conversation, some chatter about the music being written by an Italian nephew by marriage among the numerous Bassanos and Laniers. Palmer's mind was elsewhere.

He was about to make his excuses when another, grander figure hove into view. Emilia made a deep curtsey which was ignored. The figure moved past, sweeping Palmer up in his wake.

'I would not have expected to find you here. It's ... Palmer, isn't it?'

The speaker was gorgeously dressed in brocaded silk. The hair was shorter than it once was but still over-long. Palmer found himself looking at a man he had last seen in a cell in the Tower of London sentenced to death for treason after the Essex uprising. Henry Wriothesley, Earl of Southampton had plainly profited from self-reinvention since his release by King James.

He offered a pair of fingers to be touched. Palmer pretended not to see them.

'Guest of Mr Jonson,' he restricted himself to saying.

'Ah yes, everyone is a Mr now. Are you ... Palmer?'

Palmer felt his hackles rise.

'Always have been, several centuries of us in Kent ... sir.'

... which was more than could be said for the Wriothesleys, jumped up lawyers as Palmer knew perfectly well, springing into public life only two generations back when they had lengthened their name in proportion to their accumulation of money and titles.

'So, a friend of Mr Jonson ... do you still see Shakespeare?' Southampton asked, of the man who was once his own house-poet and friend.

'I believe he's now Mr Shakespeare, too,' Palmer could not resist saying. 'But no, that was business ... sir. And I am a guest of Mr Jonson, not a friend.'

'Interesting, interesting ... now, when we last ... met ... you were doing some work for our highly regarded Chief Minister....'

Palmer saw the same foxy look from the last time, the cold, glittering, grey-green eyes. He knew he was being pumped.

'Still am, sir, still am.'

'You have heard the news about one of the conspirators, Tresham? Died in the Tower just before Christmas, excruciating death, strangury, acute retention of urine in the bladder, true by all accounts. A very unhealthy place, the Tower, as we both remember. And you are retained by the Chief Minister in these latest terrible affairs?'

Poor sod, Palmer thought to himself about the highly-strung Tresham, before confirming Southampton's question, a rich one coming from the mouth of a one-time traitor.

'*Interesting,*' the Earl said, '*interesting,*' before gliding on without a backward glance, looking for finer company.

Emilia was gone too.

~ 19 ~

FTER THE HOLIDAYS, Palmer received his letter of instruction from the Chief Minister, to go to the Midlands to hunt Jesuits.

The treason trial was timed for later in the month, when the surviving insurgents would be brought to book. Palmer was not sorry to miss it. He knew all about the show of due process masking a predetermined outcome. He had seen before the standard furious performance from Attorney-General Coke as the Crown prosecutor. He knew how the story must end. He almost felt sorry for Wintour, Digby and the other survivors who now included Wintour's brother, captured after his time on the run. The news of Tresham's death in the Tower from illness had encouraged only one reaction from Palmer, that the man had been mercifully spared.

Salisbury's letter itemised the houses of the insurgents in the Warwickshire and Worcestershire borders, at the same time recommending that new hiding places be identified and searched. It made sense to the investigator – it was unlikely that the wanted Jesuits would hide in houses already known to the authorities. He knew what he would be looking for – recusant families of quiet reputation with substantial properties with scope for secret hiding places. He had come from such a family himself.

Palmer travelled by way of Oxford.

At the Town Tavern he was greeted coolly by a heavily pregnant Jane Davenant.

'I am not sure that you are welcome here, Mr Palmer. Isn't that your name?'

Palmer thought better than to deny it.

'I am sorry for the deception, Mrs Davenant, Government business.'

'As if that's any better!'

Palmer raised an eyebrow in genuine surprise.

'What traveller wants to rub up against Government informers at an inn? It doesn't do our good name any good at all!'

Palmer was tired.

'Mrs Davenant, take me as you found me when I stood godparent with you to a bastard child. I have come here to see that child.'

'There is that in your favour,' Jane Davenant conceded. 'We got your package at Christmas. Ellen was very pleased by it.'

'Is she behaving herself?'

'Ask her yourself, that's her coming now.'

Palmer was surprised at the change in the scrawny kid he had left behind. She was plumper and more confident, like someone who had found her place in life. She carried the baby in her arms.

'Thought it was you,' she said. 'I brought little Miracle to see you.'

Palmer looked at the child still tightly wrapped in yards of cloth, a small yawn indicating that she was tired and only just awake. He could not see her hair. He asked what colour it was.

'Red like her mother's,' Jane Davenant said with an affection which Palmer was pleased to hear. The child would always have a home with the Davenants.

'You got kids?' Ellen asked bluntly.

He shook his head, making no jokes about insofar as he knew. He saw Ellen's interest grow and he knew why – it increased Miracle's prospects from her mysterious godfather.

'Haven't you something to say?' Mrs Davenant reminded her servant.

'Oh yaas. Thank you for the gifts. Didn't say as 'oo they was from, but the carrier told us so we knew.'

'And is little Miracle well?' Palmer asked.

'Thrivin'.'

Palmer threw a look across to Jane Davenant, to establish whether he should stay or go.

'Put the baby back in her cradle,' the landlady told Ellen, 'and show Mr *Palmer* his chamber.'

It was a strange experience, having his feet comfortably under a family table. Seated in front of the open fire in the inn at the end of the day, Jane Davenant and Ellen on stools on either side of him, Palmer was unusually content.

'So, no kids then, as you know of,' Ellen said with a cheeky grin.

'Ellen!' Jane Davenant exclaimed.

Palmer shrugged.

'Means no woman neither,' Ellen deduced irrationally but accurately.

Palmer wondered where this was leading. He had seen plenty of examples in his time, of autumn forcing itself on spring. It had given him cases enough when it went sour as often it did. It was not something he wanted for himself.

'Was there before?'

Jane Davenant shifted her pregnant bulk expectantly on the stool.

Palmer shrugged again.

Did Emilia count, darkly beautiful, spirited, but at the core corrupt, or so he used to think? Now he didn't know.

Perhaps she was only making her way, like him, in a difficult world. Or was it the old, old story of the battle of the sexes and who would have the upper hand?

Men tried to control what they feared – was that her talking?

Everything was commodity with her. In the gardens of Kent he had not been commodity enough for the ambitious young woman she was then, and still reckoned herself to be if the association with Lady Cumberland was anything to go by.

He had come to understand commodity.

'Women's wants are not for me,' he said, gathering himself up to go to bed, leaving the women to make of him what they could.

When Palmer saddled up in the morning he made sure that Ellen and Miracle were out of the way before he spoke to Jane Davenant. He put four large coins into her hand.

'Mr Palmer!' the landlady said, looking at the golden angels. 'That's as much as a good girl's dowry round here.'

'Government employment pays well, Mrs Davenant, so you may as well have it while I've got it. Keep it, half for Ellen if she marries, the rest for Miracle.'

'Shall we be seeing no more of you?'

'I shall be back this way.'

'God willing, as my husband says.'

Palmer took the Stratford road, diverting west to Moreton. By night he had descended a steep hill into the village of Broadway on the plain, aiming for Worcester.

His instructions ordered him to meet up with the owner of nearby Holt Castle, north of the city. He was riding in its direction late the following afternoon when he came across a posse heading towards him.

Palmer presented his orders to its leader, a justice of the peace. The man was in a hurry.

'We're riding to Hindlip, a home of known recusants. We shall stay as long as it takes even if it means ripping the house apart. Any special orders from Lord Salisbury?'

'Jesuits are to be taken alive and sent to London.'

'I see, so no clumsiness like at Holbeach.'

'Something like that.'

'Well, priests don't normally offer violence but I will order my men to be careful.'

Palmer fell in with the posse behind its leader.

It was the sight of approaching horses, spotted across the open countryside which alerted the occupants of the house and drove them into a flurry of activity. Secret recesses were opened up by the women and their servants. Four men were shut in – two priests and their lay servants in separate places – only just in time.

Now came the test of silence for Father Garnet and his fellow priest inside.

They sat cramped and unmoving, hidden from sight as they listened to the bustle outside the connecting door, the raised voices and the tramp of invading boots. The capsule where they hid smelled of wood and dust. Garnet had a sudden fear – what if he sneezed? He made himself breathe evenly and shallowly. With any luck, the search would be brief, the searchers might go the same day, or the next. When they did, he would have to move on. Where to? It would be difficult. The extent of the public alert was bound to be wide.

Garnet put his trust in God.

In the hallway of the house the justice of the peace and Palmer conferred.

'How do you know that there are priests here?' Palmer asked.

'We don't, except that the family are natural suspects – recusants, previous history of anti-government activity, ideal location, big property built over the last generation with plenty of opportunities to install special features....'

'Like priest holes?'

'Yes, and we know something more. We have some of the smaller fry from the Holbeach business locked up in Worcester gaol. A couple of overheard conversations have pointed the finger in this direction.'

'So how are you going to go about things?'

'We've had a lot of advice from Whitehall, to bring in men experienced in building work so that we can check for cavities, examine the usual places – lofts, gatehouses, cellars, drill through the panelling, that sort of thing....'

'So you are prepared to take your time?'

'Yes, up to a point. Do you have anything to add?'

Palmer put himself in the position of the hideaways. They would have problems of what? Food and water, lack of space, the strength of their nerves....

'It's like a siege, Sir Henry, a matter of time, pressure, their lessening reserves, our ability to ensure they don't get any more.'

'So what would you do?'

'Exactly what you are doing. Beyond that, I would have patience, oh, and keep an eye on the women and the servants so that it's difficult for them to smuggle food and water. We have to wait the priests out. If we do, they only have three choices.'

'Which are?'

'To die where they are – then we'll smell them. To make a break for it – when we'll catch them. Or to give themselves up.'

Father Garnet, boxed inside the cubbyhole between two chimneys, was drifting towards the sin of despair. It was the third day of their incarceration. The little food there had been was gone. Some liquid nourishment came through tubes fed by the lady of the house. She did it late at night from inside her bedroom, where the Government men refused to go, despite Palmer's advice.

The Jesuits had fouled the space several times where they sat, uncomfortably cramped. There had been no time to put chamber pots in place. It was as if their bowels were concerned to rid the flesh of all bodily excess. The air was close and fetid. Despite his discomfort, Garnet made no noise. Outside, he heard the regular movements of searchers coming and going and the sounds of panelling being probed and in some cases removed. Occasionally he eased the pressure of his buttocks on the seat. He had less and less feeling in his legs and feet.

How long would it be before they got round to this area? When would the animal stink lead sensitive noses to the spot? Why were they taking so long? Had they got information? Not from the household, or the hidden would already have been discovered.

Garnet had once gone for four days in similar circumstances, but then he had been a younger man and it had almost killed him. He did not think he could do any better. Unless God intervened, their time would soon be up.

Palmer told himself to be patient.

He was encouraged when the man of the house returned home, denying too obviously all knowledge of priests and hiding holes. It was almost comical, as each hiding place was excavated and found to contain articles for the Catholic mass, how the man threw up his hands in shock at the discovery. And how he continued with his denials, until one place was found to contain the deeds to the property which were unlikely to have found their way there by magic.

No, they were onto something, Palmer was sure. It was only a matter of time.

He thanked God that his own father had died before the arrival of the Jesuits in the country. It would have been typical of the old man to harbour them. If he had, maybe something of the father's cussedness would have rubbed off onto his son. Funny how such little accidents of history turned the hunted into the hunter.

Palmer returned his mind to practical considerations. His suspicions began to centre on the gallery in the house. He had a work party sent in there under his supervision. The wall was panelled in the usual way so the men tapped on the wood, sounding for cavities. Every now and again, a gimlet was applied to pierce the wood, looking for empty space on the other side. So far the result was mouldy old plaster.

It was the fourth day of the search, a Thursday. The justice of the peace came in to inspect the progress of the work.

'Nothing so far,' Palmer confirmed.

'Then I need the men elsewhere.'

Palmer knew better than to argue. He made a last request.

'Give us a little more time.'

Sir Henry was annoyed – what had this man Palmer done for them except tell him what they already knew? Any secret cavities would already have been found by them without him. He was beginning to resent this Whitehall interference. He decided to stand on his dignity.

'No more time. The men come with me.'

The men had stopped working to watch the clash of their superiors. Palmer stayed put, watching the men troop out. Their leader waited for Palmer to follow them. He did not move. The justice turned on his heel and left.

Palmer settled down on a bench in the corner of the room. Hours passed.

The light in the gallery grew darker despite the daytime outside. A panel in the wainscotting – was it moving? Palmer had to look twice to believe it. It moved again. He sat bolt upright, pulling the knife from his boot. Quietly he slipped over to the other side of the room where he could not be seen when the wall-shakers emerged.

They were two men dressed in normal clothes.

'Stay right where you are!' he shouted in his most threatening voice.

'Of course they are Jesuit priests,' the justice snapped, penning a report to Whitehall emphasising his personal involvement in their capture.

Palmer was not nearly so sure. The two men had only admitted to being recusants. Why they would be scared enough

to wall themselves up made no sense to Palmer. They struck
him as working men, not men of the cloth. Sir Henry handed
his report to a messenger.

'Let me talk to them,' the investigator asked.

'Do what you like, for all the good it will do you!'

Palmer went straight to the room where the two captives
were being held under guard.

'Timeo danaos et dona ferentes,' he chanted at them in
Latin.

'Amen,' came the reflexive response from one of the men.

Palmer laughed.

'It's a line from Virgil, not scripture or liturgy. You had no
idea what it meant, you barely knew it was Latin! You're no
Jesuit priests, unless they're accepting illiterates these days!
Now, why would you pretend to be?'

Neither of the men replied. The answer came to Palmer.

'Because we would call off our search and take you away,
and by the time we found out....'

He hated to be made a fool of.

'Where is the priest?'

No answer came. Palmer went straight to the justice and
told him what he had found out. The man was less sure of
himself now.

'We lose nothing by giving it more time,' Palmer
suggested.

In London the trial of the surviving ringleaders in Westminster
Hall was the usual brisk affair. It was conducted in front of a
mixed bench of judges and politicians, just in case the lawyers
were tempted to stray towards justice. Leading the prosecution,
Attorney-General Coke was in his windiest form. Under his

sound and fury, the defendants threaded their rosaries or smoked. It only provoked him to louder accusations against them.

Two interested observers watched the charade, one, Jonson, there to show his loyalty to the State, the other, Shakespeare, in the hope of inspiration for his Scottish play.

They heard submissions from the authorities which left no scope for failure to convict. If one key witness, Tresham, was dead from sickness in the Tower, he had left behind a useful written confession. Thomas Wintour also admitted guilt. Indicted at the same time were Fawkes, Grant – whose damaged eyes prevented him from seeing – Rookwood, Robert Wintour and two others, one a servant. Digby was to be tried separately on the same day.

The trial went to plan. The jury verdict was swift and, unsurprisingly, unanimous. The sentence was death in its most horrific ritual form – hanging, disembowelling and butchering into four parts.

'There but for the grace of God,' Jonson said afterwards to Shakespeare in a tavern.

Over two days, the condemned men were executed in separate groups. The first went to their deaths in the churchyard of St Paul's cathedral, the second in the Old Palace yard. The authorities had chosen locations in the east and west of the capital for maximum public effect. Only half of the men on the scaffold succeeded in dying when they were hanged. The remainder were taken down from the gibbet alive to be castrated, their hearts cut out, heads struck off and the bodies carved up for public display.

Sir Everard Digby behaved the most bravely of them all. When the executioner held out and proclaimed 'the heart of a traitor!' he had just enough life left in him to gasp out 'you lie!'

The fate of Guido Fawkes was the kindest. He leapt from the ladder, breaking his neck instantly at the end of the rope, before the butchery could begin on him.

Garnet and his fellow priest were at the end of their tether in an ordeal of a different kind a hundred and more miles away. They had been hidden away for a week. Hunger had given way to a sickly pain in the gut, there was little saliva on their tongues to moisten parched lips, no urine left in them to pass or to substitute for water to drink. They sat, legs swollen and bodies stiff, among their own excrement now beginning to dry with the passage of time.

It was too much to bear.

Was the Devil on the other side of the panelling prepared to wait forever? Garnet was convinced that he was. Why would God not take him away and give his suffering servant peace? Or was it that God wanted him put to the ultimate test? Had he spared his Son? No. What sort of God was this? The priest's spirit was weak, his body weaker, he wanted to rid himself of it in some way or other even at the cost of death. The spirit would survive the flesh, that was his single, last-remaining certainty. Then let death come soon....

'Take me now, oh God!' he prayed. 'Spare me public execution.'

He was beginning to hallucinate, seeing terrible visions which were as bad as the worst punishment the State could hand out. A tiny spark of mortal hope persisted in his throbbing brain. He had not condoned or promoted treason. Surely the worst charge was concealment of the plot, against which, wasn't there some chance that intelligent men would understand, remember even the obligations of the confessional, the secrets

of which must never be revealed? He must try to live to fight
again. If not, then he must follow the example of his Saviour
Christ, he who chose not to die in a hole in the corner but in
the most public way, mounted up in front of the people. If it
came to it, so should he, so should he.

He mumbled his intention to his colleague who barely had
the strength to reply beyond a sigh of consent. One after the
other, the two men lurched out of their hole into the living
world on the other side.

They found Palmer waiting for them.

~ 20 ~

THE JOURNEY of the Jesuits back to London took place at the order of Government in Whitehall on the turn of the month into February 1606.

Palmer rode with them and the heavy guard assigned. There was no chance for him to call on the Davenants as they passed through Oxford. A part of him did not want them to see what he did. He guessed that they would hear soon enough about the grim convoy and who it contained.

Ellen saw him from a window in the servants' chamber high in the Town Tavern. She was holding her baby up to see.

'That's your rich uncle two-names down there,' she cooed, 'important man, works for the King. 'E's bringin' in bad men, busy see, or sure 'e'd come see our little Miracle.'

Beyond Oxford, the travelling party found the weather cold and damp. Garnet was still weak. For the first time the priest engaged the agent in conversation.

'Palmers were once pilgrims to the holy land....'

The investigator knew the ploy. Garnet was trying to make common ground.

'... blessed seekers of the holy places.'

'Not quite,' the investigator said, 'the word comes from the Latin, to wander abroad.'

'A scholar, Mr Palmer,' Garnet complimented him. 'Either could describe my own mission. Does that mission deserve persecution?'

'Depends on the Law.'

'And if the Law is unjust?'

'The Law is the Law.'

It was not what Palmer had thought when he studied it.

Garnet reflected in silence for a moment, before speaking.

'Catholics in England receive less tolerance than Christians do from the infidel Turks. There, we are permitted to worship publicly. Here, it must be in private.'

In truth, Palmer had little sympathy for these laws. His own family had been broken by them. But in the end, hadn't a Protestant prince in France said that Paris was worth a mass when he changed faiths to gain a throne? The Palmer estates in Kent would certainly have been worth a matins if he, not his father, had had anything to do with it.

'How is it for Protestants in Spain, or France, or Rome?' he asked.

'God's Law is greater than man's.'

'Not to the man being burned.'

'So if I am executed, it is justified because of my faith if the Law demands it?'

'No, because of your treason in compassing the death of the King.'

'And you believe that this is what I wanted?'

'I have no way of knowing. I know that you did nothing to stop it.'

'But what if I did? And believe me, I did! I tried every persuasion.'

'As a man might try to persuade another not to burgle his neighbour's house. But if he doesn't alert the authorities, then the Law must judge him.'

'I believe you understand the seal of the confessional and what it forbids me to do.'

'I also understand the ingenuity of theologians in finding other ways to achieve what is necessary. You could have let it be known to those at risk, got someone to pass the message on.'

'And betray my co-religionists and our movement?'

'Are we speaking of God's will, or yours?'

'I left it in God's hands.'

'And God has left you in ours.'

'So,' Garnet said, lowering his voice, 'you will not help me.'

Palmer thought of Fawkes whom he'd nearly warned off. What was the difference? Helping Fawkes might have been a matter of fraternity, a thing of human feeling rather than godly principle. For this reason, he did not feel the same way about Garnet.

Palmer helped deliver the prisoners to the Gatehouse Prison in Westminster.

From Salisbury's official, he heard about the executed insurgents. Around the city there was a fresh outbreak of plague. People would die who did not deserve to, but they would die just the same. Catesby and his sort had at least had a choice in the matter of their own fates.

'Only Tesimond has escaped the net,' Salisbury said when Palmer got to see him; the Yorkshire priest had made it to the continent.

'What will happen to Garnet and the others?' Palmer asked.

'The pair of assistants you caught are expendable. There's been a call to send the lesser priest back to Worcester.'

Palmer was not surprised. The justice of the peace would want his public triumph, Worcester a Jesuit of its own for the theatre of the scaffold.

'A priest praying in an alien tongue at the foot of the gibbet is always an excellent way to stoke up the anger of the people.'

'And Garnet?'

'Too valuable to be broken on the rack. We shall interrogate him over and over again for all the intelligence we can get from him.'

'So he may live?'

'He will twist and turn, use all his way with words. But we want him to do just that – let him be seen to be anything other than plain and simple. We want his shiftiness and deceit made plain for all the world to see. If he tries their tactic of equivocation – which they have down to a fine art, let me tell you, we have studied some of their papers on it – then so much the better. Coke may be a bully, but he's also sharp. He will make mincemeat of anyone playing around with the meaning of words. What Garnet cannot escape is this – he knew but he did not say.'

Palmer asked when Garnet's trial was expected to take place. Not until the next month, he was told. Was there anything he should be doing in the meantime?

Salisbury cocked his head in thought.

'Keep an eye on Mr Jonson. His anxiety to help has not extended to giving up his troublesome religion. I hear he's been hauled up for recusancy and is busy ducking and weaving over the charge – as ever.'

The order appeared to give the politician pause for thought.

'What we need is consistency from our writers,' he said. 'I was saying as much to the Master of the Revels the other day. Important work, his, not least the censorship part. Yes, keep in touch with Jonson and the rest of the acting trade.'

It was not the task Palmer wanted. Then again, Jonson liked a drink and if Salisbury was happy to pay, who was Palmer to show ingratitude?

He found Jonson in fiery form at the Mermaid later that evening.

'What in God's name – literally – what has it got to do with the authorities how I worship? They had the nerve – the nerve – to say that if I don't change my ways I must start producing certificates of communion and spend my time in cosy religious chats with well-meaning old clerical fumblers boring on about the path to righteousness! I was called up in front of the beak with my wife in tow. Well, she's a sharp-tongued besom at the best of times, mother of my children – fair enough – kids who I'm pretty sure are mine, but the idea of me being responsible for her moral welfare ... I do my best to avoid living with her and the family as it is!'

'The Chief Minister is looking for you writers to support the cause,' Palmer said, passing the message on.

'It's not our job! Our job is art and amusement. Difficult to achieve any of that if you self-censor what you write. Whoever heard of a kind joke? It must be at *someone's* expense.'

Palmer ordered more beer. It lubricated Jonson's anger.

'So I write what I want and set it in another country which means that although the subject is as bold as London brass, I can say, "Oh no, it's all about these foreigners." I shouldn't be here,' he sighed, contradicting himself with a wistful look at his beermug. 'I've work to do.'

He took a deep draught instead.

'... by the way, I did think about that Scotch mist you told me about, the three Sybils and all the rest of it, but it wasn't for me. I put our friend Shakespeare onto it.'

'Did you now? What's he up to these days?'

Palmer liked to keep his ear to the ground when it came to troublemakers.

'Being a good King's Man,' was all Jonson would say.

February turned into March.

Palmer had little to do, other than wait for the trial of the Jesuit, Henry Garnet. At last he heard the date – March 28th at the Guildhall in the City, chosen for maximum effect in the most populous part of the capital.

'Garnet's been interrogated more than twenty times,' Salisbury's official confided to him.

Palmer knew what that meant. He heard without surprise that one of the two assistants to Garnet had died from torture – suicide, the Government claimed.

'A statement made when interrogation is too enthusiastic,' the official explained.

On his way home to his new lodging, Palmer was halted in his tracks. Familiar signs were marked on doors.

'Plague,' a man said, one of a party bringing out bodies and sealing up rooms.

Could a man be infected twice? Palmer was not about to experiment. He turned on his heel and headed towards his old tenement slum where his rent was still in credit. There, in the old family bed, despite the dark and the smell, he knew that he had come home.

21

'I HAVE SET OUT in every detail the many treasons which you have provoked – and organised – in your secret mission to subvert this kingdom from its faith and loyalty.'

The accuser, Attorney-General Coke was casting his net long and wide. Palmer had seen him do it before. He looked round him in the courtroom. He saw a familiar face – Shakespeare's.

'We come now to your hideous practice of equivocation.'

Garnet stood in a dock which had been specially raised to give the watching public the best view of the man described as the Devil incarnate. He looked anything but – pale and slight and weak from nearly two months of incarceration and interrogation. With his glasses and his thinning hair, he looked to Palmer more like an inoffensive schoolmaster than a diabolic, blinking while Coke thundered on.

'We have heard that you and your confederates, to all outward appearances, condemn lying and perjury. Yet isn't it the truth that what you condemn in others, you practice when it serves your own purposes, *and,*' the prosecutor went on quickly to cut off any answer to his own rhetorical question, 'we lay as evidence a treatise found in the possession of the late traitor, Francis Tresham. This wicked document talks openly of "dissimulation", the use of words to change their real meaning so that, on the face of it, *the bare-faced lying* face of it, no lie or perjury can be heard to be committed!'

Palmer shut his eyes as Coke's speech roiled around the courtroom. The prosecutor was going for the throat – Government was not content with the charge of concealment of treason, it had to have the living Garnet as treason's author now that Catesby was dead.

What was the phrase the lawyers used, translated from the Latin?

'The author is more guilty than the actor.'

Palmer's eye returned to William Shakespeare.

There were parallels, Palmer reflected. Garnet had already protested in the trial – when Coke allowed him to speak – that Catesby's hypothesis about means and ends had been completely obscure to him in the house by the river. The two men, Garnet and Shakespeare, the one a paid retainer of the State, the other its enemy, had a lot in common in their manipulation of words.

'We come to Francis Tresham's letter of confession before his death,' Coke announced. 'Now we have heard from Mr Garnet ... and others ... that he had several times met Tresham over the last two years. Yet what does Tresham say, on his deathbed, what does this student of equivocation say? That he had not seen Mr Garnet, and I quote, "for fifteen or sixteen years". What are we to make of that, other than that even as he lay dying, he was manifestly lying, and lying in the way he was taught to? Is that not so, Mr Garnet? *Is that not so?*'

Garnet was heard clearing his throat. Palmer could see what had happened – poor Tresham had tried to exonerate the priest as his last act. The irony was that his motive for lying was pure. The Jesuit in the dock looked, all of a sudden, badly tired.

'It may be that he meant to equivocate....'

... trying to preserve the truth of his, Garnet's innocence, but the words would not come, they stuck in the Jesuit's throat.

Coke smiled, an alarming sight. The rictus disappeared as quickly as it had come.

'We turn now to the matter of the seal of the confessional,' he said. 'Now, the accused says that he was bound by the seal of the confessional not to reveal what was confessed to him. Yet even in the canon law of the old, discredited faith, this is simply wrong. What was communicated to the priest was not something which had been done, but which was a future action, something yet to be done, as yet unexecuted....'

'And we know,' interrupted one of the politicians sitting in judgement, 'that what a man does not stop when he can, he authorises.'

Palmer remembered arguing the same with Garnet on the road back from Oxford. He heard a third voice raised in the court. It was Salisbury's.

'And I would add, my lords, that even if there were such a thing as the seal of the confessional justifying concealment, the confession made was not privileged in this way. As I understand it, confession has to be followed by contrition and amendment. Since the traitor Catesby was in no way contrite – he did not afterwards desist from his evil act, he never repented it – therefore his confession was invalid and so his confessors were released from the seal; if it exists at all, which, as I said, I tend to deny.'

A ripple of approval ran around the court at this filigree reasoning. Salisbury was not finished.

'Moreover, the hypothesis raised by Catesby, about the death of innocents, was not, nor has it ever been claimed to be, in confession. The accused therefore is not protected by the seal of confession when he realised what Catesby was proposing.'

It was like watching a chicken being expertly trussed and then stuffed, Palmer thought.

Garnet cleared his throat again.

'I must repeat that I did not understand what was meant in the conversation and that later, when I did, I did everything in my power to prevent....'

The last word went unheard.

In a secret room off the courtroom looking out onto it, King James sat looking on, fascinated by the cross-examination. He was pleased that his Chief Minister had consulted him on the framing of the precise questions to be put to the priest of Rome. There was one in particular that he had personally spent time getting absolutely right. He heard it now, rehearsed in court.

'Is, by your doctrine, a priest bound to reveal a dangerous treason if communicated to him in confession when the party confessing indicates his determination to persist in the action?'

Garnet was silent for some moments. At last he spoke.

'The party cannot be absolved unless he submits himself....'

To what, Palmer wondered, to self-prohibition, or simply to penance for his intended action? The answer was not entirely clear.

'... on the other hand, the confessor must use all lawful means to hinder the treason, which I maintain is what I did.'

The answer fell on unconvinced ears – the carefully picked jury of London businessmen were not the sort to be impressed by finer theological points.

Their verdict of guilty barely justified their retirement to consider it.

Palmer put himself in Shakespeare's way as the crowd disgorged from the trial.

'Ah, Mr Palmer,' Shakespeare said without any warmth.

'I hear that you are busy with a Scottish play,' Palmer said as citizens flooded past them, most in happy, holiday mood, looking forward to the forthcoming execution announced by the court.

Shakespeare was not going to answer. The statement was true, but he had revealed its title to nobody in case someone else tried to beat him to it – one couldn't be too careful in the cutthroat writing business. He restricted himself to a nodded acceptance of the fact and wondered how he could get away from Salisbury's agent as quickly as possible.

'And does it have a title?' Palmer persisted.

'In the theatre, Mr Palmer, it's bad luck to talk about an unperformed work. Foolish of us, perhaps, but we think it's tempting Fate.'

Palmer didn't think it was foolish at all. As a man who had no cause to believe in God, he entirely accepted the will or whim of Fate. It explained poor old Garnet's situation.

'Now if you will pardon me,' Shakespeare said, brushing past.

It was well into April before Palmer was admitted to see his client Salisbury again. The Easter festival was well advanced, and the recent outbreak of plague seemed to have subdued itself. Palmer was back in his old lodgings. He could not bring himself to return to the comforts of the smarter chamber in the former monastery, whatever was said about the plague being over.

He found the Chief Minister in good form.

'It's all been so very satisfactory. The plot and its ringleaders have been crushed, we've finally done for the chief Jesuit and his underground network – those that aren't dead are in prison – and we've mopped up a cluster of suspect Catholic peers.'

'What is going to happen to Northumberland?' Palmer asked, about the biggest fish caught, fairly or not, in the net cast over the insurgency.

Salisbury chuckled, a rare sound in itself.

'The noble Earl is to stand trial – this is confidential, not everyone is behind the idea.'

'And the charge?'

'Seeking to become the leader of the English Papists and to obtain formal toleration for them. As I have told you before, toleration and tolerance are, in His Majesty's mind two very different things. Northumberland *has* been rather careless. You see, as head of the King's bodyguard....'

'Wasn't Thomas Percy one?'

'Yes, and there's the rub – our noble lord failed to have Percy swear the oath of loyalty to the King above all others. You can imagine His Majesty's regard for someone who allowed an unsworn bodyguard within striking distance of him.'

The hapless Earl stood next to no chance of survival, thought Palmer.

Salisbury appeared to read his mind.

'His Majesty is the most merciful of rulers. Should the trial of Northumberland return a verdict of guilty on any of the counts, then I suspect that the Earl can expect to be a guest of His Majesty in the Tower for the rest of his days. If that were the case, then I expect that the Crown would be recompensed by a heavy fine on the Earl's estate.'

It was already a done deal, Palmer reckoned, of the usual profitable sort.

'Yes, His Majesty is most content with the way things have turned out,' Salisbury said, 'a small measure of which can be seen in his great benevolence to me, humble servant though I be.'

More gravy for the over-served, Palmer was not slow to realise, but what else could there be for Salisbury to want? It was less than a year since his receipt of an earldom, the highest rank of nobility outside the royal family. What else was there?

'I am to be appointed Knight of the Garter.'

Palmer suppressed a whistle of surprise. Membership of the ancient order, the most personal gift the monarch could bestow was generally restricted to fellow princes in Europe and to the oldest nobility. The Cecils were new men.

'I want some of that benevolence to be shared with those who have done good service to the State,' Salisbury said with a smile, 'men like you, Dick.'

Gravy for me too, Palmer thought, despite being irked at the use of the diminutive. He was all ears.

'My proposal is this....'

Walking away from Whitehall, Palmer did not know what he felt about Salisbury's offer. He needed a drink.

He walked along the Strand, past the mansions of the great including that of the soon-to-be- unfortunate Northumberland. He passed the Irish Boy, where Jonson had introduced him to Catesby. He kept on walking, through Ludgate, up to St Paul's to find his regular drinking den, the Bell on Carter Lane. He took a stool and ordered beer.

His friend the landlord came to sit with him.

'Looks as you've 'ad news,' the landlord began, not knowing whether he should be ready to commiserate or congratulate.

'Chief Minister's offered me a job.'

'Oh yes,' the landlord said, none the wiser.

'It's in the office of the Master of the Revels. He's apparently on the way out. There's a deputy waiting to take over.'

'Who's he?'

'Doesn't matter ... he's in line to step up, in fact he's already paid for the privilege. When the present man finally goes for good – in a year or two – the deputy will move up and a vacancy will be created.'

'So what's this Master of the Revels do then? Sounds lively to me.'

'He organises the Court entertainments. He supervises them and books the performers, for example the acting companies.'

'The actors, eh?'

The landlord was immediately suspiciously. He found it difficult to believe that such roughnecks would be allowed near the Court. He'd had a few in the Bell in his time; always kept a close eye on them, for drinking and whoring and not paying for any of it.

'Well, you've had a fair crack at revellin' in your time.'

'Ah, but that's not the job.'

'So what is it, then?'

'The Revels office licences the public plays. It checks out all the scripts, the words, before they are performed. The office reports to the Lord Chamberlain.'

The landlord was impressed. Palmer wished that he himself could be. He cast his mind back to Salisbury's words in making him the offer. Salisbury had been flattering.

'You have a good understanding of the world of the theatre without being too familiar with its practitioners. You also have the right attitude, and we shouldn't forget that you are an educated man, a graduate of our old college at Cambridge.'

He accepted all of that. What filled him with dread was the prospect of life locked away inside some poky cubbyhole surrounded by paper. Even worse was the idea of reading and marking the paperwork, for censorship was part of what was involved, as the Chief Minister had gone to the trouble of explaining. All that greasy contact with the actors!

'How'd you make your money?' the landlord asked.

'Those who submit plays for scrutiny pay a fee.'

'I see. So you needs 'em as much as they needs you.'

It was an uncomfortably good way of putting it, Palmer thought.

'I don't have to decide immediately,' Palmer said. 'The post doesn't need to be filled for a while, though there would need to be time spent learning the ropes, before the change of the guard.'

'Best o' both worlds, sounds like to me,' the landlord decided as he called for more beer for his upwardly-moving customer.

You never could tell which way fortune might shift in these fast-changing times.

22

I T WAS a special treat for the public to enjoy the execution of the Jesuit Henry Garnet on the first Saturday in May, a public holiday. The scaffold was set up in St Paul's churchyard in the heart of the city, a public concourse for the doing of business legal and illegal. It was the home to bookstalls, taverns and eating places; and to the comings and goings of people for whom the yard was the short cut to somewhere else – Garnet included, Palmer reckoned privately as he found himself a place in the crowd.

Shakespeare and Jonson had already taken their places together in the holiday gathering. Neither was a frequenter of public executions. Jonson had once narrowly avoided his own, after killing a fellow actor. Shakespeare was there to keep an eye on his volatile friend who was determined to attend, rashly to his mind, to support Garnet in his final agony.

Jonson was nervous.

'Some way to make your first public appearance on the stage!'

Shakespeare understood. Garnet was cast to play the biggest scene in his life as the greatest public enemy of the day. He would know the hideousness of what was to follow, and how the way that he bore it would shape the verdict of the world on himself and on his Catholic faith. It made the world of plays and players seem very small in comparison.

Garnet lay on his back shivering in anticipation. The hurdle onto which he was strapped, a wicker sled drawn by horses, was approaching the end of its journey. He could hear the noise of the crowd grow and then surge as he came nearer, his hands clasped in piety (and to stop them trembling), his face looking up to the skies as he lay, tied down on his back, dragged along the ground. He prayed for the courage to withstand the public hatred of him, and the brutal butchering. He did not feel ready for martyrdom or sainthood.

'This is as far as he goes,' Jonson whispered to Shakespeare out of the side of his mouth as the cortege approached.

Garnet sensed a slowing to a stop. Men appeared above him, blotting out most of the sky and its puffs of white clouds chasing across the blue beyond. Was that where he was going, afterwards? Where was Heaven? His mind drifted towards theological speculation. Strong hands shook him out of it, unbinding him and pulling him roughly to his feet. He was pleased to find that he could stand without too much difficulty. He felt himself being half-pushed, half-guided towards the scaffold and its steps. He mounted them cautiously, the noise of the crowd rising with his own unsteady ascent, rung by careful rung.

It was as if they were shouting at someone else. His limbs were not used to exercise, not in recent months. He made it to the top with relief, breathing hard. He could feel the thump of his heart from the exertion. It was strange to him to think that this organ would be stopped in a matter of minutes, ripped out in order to achieve just that for his and for the public view.

'Such a reception for him!' Jonson muttered.

Four men were waiting, the senior law officer, a judge and two religious leaders.

Garnet sighed at the prospect of one more scene to be played out before the climax of his drama. His body might be ready but this was a terrible intrusion, to assault his peace of mind. The law officer spoke, loudly so that the assembly could hear. There was politics still to be resolved.

'I ask you now to reveal any other acts of treason you may have committed or of which you have secret knowledge.'

Garnet looked around him. It was an expectant audience which stood below, or sat in spectator stands, or hung out of the upper windows of houses nearby like some vast theatrical crowd. It was a huge gathering to be drawn by the fate of one man. His mind turned, before he dismissed the thought as unworthy, to Christ's sermon on the mount.

'Blessed are the meek' ... it lent determination to his reply.

'I have nothing more to add.'

His voice was humble, but it carried, floated upwards by him with his years of experience of ministry.

The two religious leaders stepped forward to argue their creed against his.

Pathetic, Jonson thought, that they had to have the last word even as they were putting the man to death, like terriers arguing over a cornered rat. Garnet cut them short and asked to be allowed a little time, and space, to say his prayers in his own way.

The law officer persisted in badgering the Jesuit for further admissions. Garnet refused to give way. The law officer lost this temper.

'You're no more than equivocating!'

Enough to equivocate himself to heaven or not, Shakespeare wondered, this man who had, in the public mind, committed treason for his God's sake?

'Enough! Have you anything more to say?'

Garnet composed himself, clearing his throat.

'Today is the day on which the True Cross of Christ was found, and on this day I thank God that I have found my own cross.'

The words gave him back belief, enough to reconcile himself to his fate. There was something important he had to say. He gathered his forces.

'I am guilty of no treason. I feel horror that some of my faith attempted such an action. I ask them, now, to live quietly and peaceably and...' his voice broke for a moment before he could go on, 'God will not forget them,' as he quietly prayed that he would not forget him.

He was finished. He made his way to the foot of the ladder to pray, then he mounted the ladder with awkward steps. At the top, he prayed again, commending his spirit to the Lord and to Mary, Mother of Grace and Mercy. The words, in the Latin banned for so many years from religious use and only recited clandestinely before the faithful, seemed to bloom in the open air. Garnet's voice grew in confidence. Finally he crossed his arms across his chest.

He felt the ladder give way and go, and suffocating pain, and strong hands pulling hard on his feet and legs to make the agony shorter.

A line came into Shakespeare's mind, about life as a tale told by an idiot, signifying nothing.

The day after, Richard Palmer was on horseback inside the city walls at Oxford making for the Town Tavern.

He found another addition to the family once he had stabled his horse. The baby's face peering out of a mass of linen was round, lusty and the apple of his mother's, Jane Davenant's eye.

'He's two months old now,' she told Palmer proudly as she presented the boy to him. 'We called him William.'

For the actor-godfather.

He found Ellen in the kitchen. Inside a swivel-hoop he saw a bundle of energy, held up on rubbery legs as she staggered about in narrow arcs proscribed by the metal contraption which governed her. Miracle looked to be a happy child.

'Nine months old,' Ellen tutted, 'an' crawls everywhere if we doesn't keep a look out for her. Still, she 'as a nice little playmate now.'

Palmer surprised himself by going over and lifting the baby gently out of the hoop. Little Miracle did not cry. Ellen looked pleased. Palmer handed the child over to her mother, happy to quit while he was in credit.

That evening, the Davenants entertained Palmer to supper. There was news, inevitably, to tell them from London. Palmer said nothing about his own part in the events. It was a relief when he found himself talking about the offer from the Chief Minister to work for the Master of the Revels.

Jane Davenant was impressed.

'And you will accept?'

Palmer shrugged.

John Davenant signalled speech with his pipe.

'Way I look at it is this ... one godfather writes the stuff, t'other crosses some of it out. Should make for a convenient world ... God willing.'

~ 23 ~

THE GLOBE was packed to the rafters for the new Scottish play, thrilled by rumours that it was to tackle the recent political scares. Weren't the actors the King's Men, surely they must know, or have heard, or have seen things not given to ordinary folk?

The crowd was to be close-at-hand witness to a high drama of State. Expectation ran wild. A full house seethed with the excitement which came from presence at something sure to be remarkable, worth telling others, now and in times to come.

Palmer did not share the general enthusiasm. He was back on duty for the dried up old Alderman in the case of his flighty young wife, now that both had returned from the country to the plague-free city. He didn't need the money, but it was something to do and it kept his capital intact in the hands of the goldsmith on Cheapside. It was beer money, a good position to be in.

The gossip going on around him was full of the wonders of 'our glorious King'. Palmer had heard it in the streets and drinking houses as well. It crossed his mind that this was the last thing the insurgents would have predicted, the elevation of the Scots King to public affection for the first time in his three-year reign.

He settled as best he could on the bench in an upper gallery. From there he could observe the Alderman's wife and her friends at a lower level opposite. They were surrounded by men on the make, free with their smiles and their hands which the women accepted or rejected as they chose. Palmer had an extra motive as well. Today would help him decide on the censorship job which he had not yet accepted.

The sound of mechanical thunder quelled the noise among the audience.

'When shall we three meet again....'

Three witches scuttled onto and round the stage dressed in hooded rags. The audience quieted, subdued by what they saw, these creatures of the supernatural in which most of them believed.

Battle reports flowed in proclaiming victory for a general successful in repulsing the attack of foreign invaders. The audience fell silent in anticipation as the company's leading actor strode out onto the stage. Burbage was their man for the big part.

The witches hailed him by name – 'Macbeth.' Prophecy was their purpose, to the general and to his comrade–in–arms whom they called Banquo. Palmer instantly recognised the name, from the Latin play in Oxford. So this was the ancestor of the Stuarts. He eased forward on his bench with a closer, censor's interest.

'Lesser than Macbeth and greater.'

Spectators spread the meaning to those who had not yet grasped it – Banquo would be the founder of a royal line represented today by good, brave King James. Someone was seeding a message.

There was nothing to worry a censor so far, everything in fact to please.

The entrance of Macbeth's wife drew gesticulations of excitement from someone in particular. It was the Alderman's wife in the gallery below. What did that mean? Palmer looked more closely at the figure onstage. This wasn't the blond-wigged sweet innocent, the boy who had played the young wife offered up on a bed of a black man's jealousy the last time Palmer was forced to frequent the place. This was a harpy, nurtured in ruthlessness, with a mature male voice, high and swooping.

'Come, you spirits
That tend on mortal thoughts, unsex me here!'

Ripe laughter from the admiring women around the Alderman's wife greeted the demand. No, it wasn't a boy onstage, it was a young man whose words had another meaning as far as the women were concerned. An idea lodged in Palmer's mind as to just who it was, recalled from that first case of his when Shakespeare was in trouble in the time of the old Queen.

'Look like the innocent flower, but be the serpent under it,' Lady Macbeth urged her husband.

The serpent, that's what the prosecution had accused Garnet of being, Palmer remembered. Whatever the Macbeths were up to, it must lead to murder. But there was no justification for the deed. Macbeth on the stage far below intoned the virtues of his intended victim. Palmer imagined another king, James, basking in pleasure at the claim. The author was leaving no room for doubt that he was, everyone was, without doubt, the King's Man.

Cheers from the spectators greeted a favourite comic weaving out onto the stage. A satirical game of 'knock knock' started with urgent fists banged on the castle doors. This porter was a low character and Scots too.

'Faith, here's an equivocator, that could swear in both scales against either scale; who committed treason enough for God's sake, yet could not equivocate to heaven.'

A grunt of approval registered among the watchers at the reference to Garnet, followed by the first applause of the afternoon.

The time came for Banquo to die at the hands of murderers recruited by Macbeth. Risky, Palmer-as-censor thought, assassinating the Stuart ancestor onstage. And totally against the classical rules of drama....

The murderer-for-hire set out his stall, as 'one whom the vile blows and buffets of the world hath so incensed that I am reckless what I do to spite the world.'

Catesby, and others like him?

Banquo fell under a flurry of knife-blows in front of his infant son. The mood of the audience turned grim. Where else recently had a royal father and son risked being murdered together?

When Banquo's son escaped, they shouted their support. When Banquo's ghost returned to haunt Macbeth at a royal banquet, they murmured at the apparition, remembering another ghost, of a murdered king in a Danish play, and guessing at awful consequences to follow.

Macbeth descended into infernal depths to consult the witches about the future succession to the throne – nothing for the line of Macbeth.

A child bantered with his mother, another pair marked down for death.

Lady Macbeth went mad with guilt, and went away to die. There was little sympathy from the crowd.

Climactic conflict between the forces of good and evil brought the play back into line. Palmer tolerated the marching and countermarching, the blare of trumpets and the clash of steel as pockets of men pretended to be thousands. Revenging Scots and English allies – more symbols of James's unifying stance – advanced from wood to castle to overthrow the tyrant. A restored prince showered promotions on his supporters as a liberal monarch should, as King James of Scotland had, in his case from liberal English wealth.

The final applause, when it came, was generous. The crowd began to funnel out of the playhouse, full of satisfaction at the morality play they thought they had seen. But Palmer noticed that the Alderman's wife and her friends were not leaving with them. They reappeared close to the actors' entrance from the tiring house at the back of the stage. Palmer went downstairs towards them.

A familiar voice stopped him in his tracks.

'Mr Palmer! So your fascination with the theatre hasn't exhausted itself?'

Shakespeare laughed, his strange, explosive whoop. Next to him stood Ben Jonson.

An old pugnacity stirred itself in Palmer. He marched towards the provocation. He saw Jonson squaring up in case there was a brawl, caught the look of anticipation in his eyes. Suddenly, he felt the anger desert him.

'All in a day's work,' he said, 'and my compliments to your Lady Macbeth – your brother, Edmund, isn't it? From man to woman, and then so potently back to man,' he said, seeing the actor emerge to enjoy the attentions of his female admirers.

Keep your hands off my brother, Shakespeare's lips smiled.

'It's custom on the stage,' his lips said.

'Or in life,' Jonson added, as Ned Shakespeare pressed his lips on the exposed bosom of the Alderman's wife among the squawks and giggles of her friends.

'Well, I should be on my way,' Palmer said, 'unless I can stand you gentlemen a drink?'

Jonson looked eager, Shakespeare decisively not.

'Mr Palmer, we have nothing to talk about.'

'Oh, I don't know.'

'We here,' said Shakespeare, 'are only actors, mere shadows. What could we possibly have to share with a figure of such substance as you are?'

Palmer smiled.

'You never can tell,' he replied.

~ Closing the File ~

'SO, YOU TAKIN' this revellin' job or not?' the landlord at the Bell Inn asked Palmer.

Palmer gave a stubborn shrug. He wasn't the only one proving obstinate according to his old contact, Salisbury's chief official.

'Old Dame Catesby,' Robin Catesby's mother, 'is fighting tooth and nail for her grandson's inheritance,' the official had told him. 'Tresham's estate is safe, but it goes to his spendthrift brother, so it will not last long.'

All the rest would be ruined – the Digbys, the Grants, the Rookwoods, the Wintours, the Wrights – the Government would see to it, unless the children were taken into the care of the State and converted from the religion of their fathers. This Palmer knew only too well – the powers-that-be took a wicked pleasure in remoulding the heirs of their enemies.

Sometimes it worked, sometimes it didn't.

As for the Percys, their chief, Northumberland found himself immured in the Tower for the foreseeable future, reduced to alchemical experiments to keep himself entertained. At least his wealth bought him comfortable lodging, or so the old official had said. The flexibly evasive Lord Mordaunt proved unable to escape a massive fine, imprisonment and ruin. Lord Monteagle, on the other hand, was a hero, busy making money through merchant ventures to Virginia and East India. It kept him profitably out of politics.

Were Jesuits to be kept out of England? Unlikely, Palmer reckoned. Already Father Tesimond's memoirs of his adventures were recruiting fresh volunteers. Did he see regret in the old official's weak eyes, now that there could be no coming

217

out for him in the twilight of his days, no re-emergence of his old faith into the glow of official toleration?

'King James has never been more safe upon the Throne,' the old official had said, parroting the Government line.

It meant Robert, Earl of Salisbury was secure too. He was growing higher and higher in influence, equal to the personal debts he was piling up keeping pace with his royal master. There was irony in this, to Palmer's eye from what the old official had told him since the Chief Minister was spending much of his time trying to control royal overspending. James really didn't have the knack of dealing with Parliament, not the way Elizabeth had.

What did it matter, Palmer asked himself? The Stuarts were unbudgeable, weren't they, after recent events? It would take something massive to threaten their hold on the Throne.

As for those on the royal gravy train, Ben Jonson was about to land the Chief Minister's sponsorship for some fancy royal entertainment, Palmer had been told. Shakespeare was still pumping out his plays, bleaker and bleaker stuff by all accounts. There were rumours that his acting company was looking to add another bow to its string – a private theatre in Blackfriars in addition to the Globe. Their attempt ten years before had been blocked by local residents.

'But they are the *King's* Men now,' the official had reminded them both. Who these days would risk offending *him*?

Palmer could not resist asking for news of Emilia Lanier. The old official's eyes had sparkled mischievously.

'I hear she is writing devotional verse among a circle of high-minded ladies.'

As the night drew on in the Bell Inn, Palmer looked back up at the landlord who was still waiting for his answer. A job in the censor's office, taking on the plays and their players? Now maybe *there* was an apple-cart worth upsetting...

Lightning Source UK Ltd.
Milton Keynes UK
UKOW02f2306070317
296047UK00001B/51/P